Never Been Kissed

"Okay," Anita said. "If you've never kissed a guy, we got big problems here."

"I've kissed guys," Josie said defensively. "I've just never *kissed* a guy. Felt that thing—"

"'That thing'?" Cynthia hooted. "Is that what you kids are calling it these days?"

Josie blushed and shook her head. How could she explain to them what she meant? "That thing. That moment. You kiss someone, and it's like the world around you gets all hazy and the only thing in focus is you and this other person, and you know that one person is the person you're meant to be kissing the rest of your life."

Never Been Kissed

Never Been Kissed

Novelization by
Cathy East Dubowski

Based on the screenplay by
Jenny Bicks, Abby Kohn, & Marc Silverstein

HarperEntertainment
A Division of HarperCollins*Publishers*

HarperEntertainment
A Division of HarperCollins*Publishers*
10 East 53rd Street, New York, NY 10022–5299

For information address HarperCollins Publishers Inc., 10 East 53rd Street, New York, NY 10022–5299.

ISBN 0-06-102013-3

First printing: May 1999

Printed in the United States of America

10 9 8 7 6 5 4 3 2 1

Never Been Kissed

1

Josie Geller was scared out of her wits.

Who wouldn't be?

She stood on the pitcher's mound of a Chicago high-school baseball stadium under the night-game lights in front of a record-breaking crowd.

Without a ball. In fact, she'd never played a game of baseball in her life. She was the ultimate benchwarmer, a girl who spent twenty-five years on the sidelines of the game.

But tonight she'd thrown herself out onto the playing field of life. And the crowds had come out to watch.

People overflowed the stands. They jammed the parking lot. They stood on the rooftops of the nearby buildings. They sat on the hoods of their cars and listened with their radios turned up loud.

Yeah, there was a high-school championship game scheduled for tonight. But the crowds hadn't come to see that.

They were there to see her. To be with her. To cheer her on.

"JOSIE! JOSIE! JOSIE!"

Or to see her make a total fool of herself.

It was a big deal for a girl who had spent most of her life trying *not* to be noticed.

None of this was supposed to happen. She was just trying to do her job. Two months ago you wouldn't have picked her out of the crowd.

And then things happened.

Life happened.

Now the game clock was set at 5:00.

Five minutes and ticking.

2

Two months earlier

Josie Geller wove her way through the maze of desks and cubicles known as the bullpen at the *Chicago Sun-Times* on her way to her office. A young copy assistant named Rhoda trailed her, holding a reporter's tablet and pen. "Theater—"

"Standard American spelling calls for *e-r*," Josie responded distractedly. "Standard British is *r-e*. So go for *e-r*—unless you're a pompous American; then go for British."

Josie Geller was a copy editor. A lot of people didn't even know what that was. Or care. Those who did thought Josie caught typos, did something to make the verbs line up right, and basically functioned as a human spell-checker. But there was more to it than that.

To Josie editing was like polishing silver—it brought out the shine. Words used the right way could start a revolution, or win somebody's heart.

And, she had to admit, it was delightful to be an authority on something about which most people, even professional writers, were clueless.

"No. Theater. Last night," Rhoda said. "We were supposed to go. Remember?"

Josie didn't answer because she had paused at the desk where Merkin Burns, office assistant, sat picking his nose as he talked on the phone. *God, what a disgusting toad.* He was supposed to work for her, among others, but somehow he always made her feel as if *she* were the one begging for *his* approval. She waited politely—more politely than he deserved. She tried to catch his eye. She cleared her throat.

Merkin continued to ignore her. "No way. No way. No *way*!" he said into the phone.

Josie tried waving.

Merkin responded with a withering look of irritation before he told his caller, "Eh! Hold on." He covered the mouthpiece and glared at her. "What."

"Messages?" Josie asked.

Merkin rolled his eyes as he snatched up a single pink message slip and held it out to her.

One measly message? Josie thought, envying the stacks she saw on the desk for other staff members.

Wrinkling her nose, she reached out and took it by one tiny corner—hoping she wouldn't get booger germs all over her. "Oh, and Merkin—"

But Merkin had swiveled in his chair, returning to his obviously important phone call. "Seriously?" he shrieked. "No way. No *way*—"

Josie kept standing there. Waiting. Maybe she'd try glaring a hole through the back of his shirt. Maybe that would get through to him.

Merkin whirled around. *"What?"*

"Merkin, do you think we could get some more yellow Hi-Liters? I checked the box, and we're—"

Merkin huffed in disgust, swung his chair around so that his back was to Josie, and continued his call. "Okay, I'm back, so . . . "

Josie sighed. What did a girl have to do around here to get office supplies? *Ask for them, instead of beg, maybe,* a little voice told her.

"Shut up," she grumbled back at the little voice as she stomped toward her office, fuming. She'd type up a memo, that's what she'd do. Maybe he'd give her a little more respect when he got the request on her office stationery.

At the door to her office she stopped to admire the nameplate:

JOSIE GELLER, COPY EDITOR

She loved seeing it etched there in crisp, straight capitals. No typos, of course. Hanging just a little crooked. With the tip of her finger she nudged the right-hand corner up just a smidge. . . . There, much better. Then she trudged into the small cozy box she called her office.

Once inside, she held up her lone phone-message slip and read it hopefully—but it was nothing, just a note from her super to let her know he'd fixed her dripping bathroom faucet. Big news. She gladly dropped the germy pink paper into the wastebasket. After placing her purse and tote bag on the chair by her desk, she neatly hung up her coat on the back of the door, then did what she always did, every morning. She removed five pencils from her pencil pot, sharpened them one by one in the electric sharpener till the red light blinked on, indicating a perfect point, then laid them out neatly on her desktop, leaving just enough room for the typed pages she would soon be marking up with corrections, queries, and suggestions. A sharp eye and a sharp pencil were the tools of her trade.

She smiled as she sat down at her desk. Everything was in order. She was ready to face another day.

And then the door burst open, and her friend Anita Brandt exploded into the room.

Josie, used to it, sighed but didn't blink.

"Guess who I did it with last night?" Anita gushed.

"Roger in op-ed."

"Who told?"

"You did." Anita couldn't keep secrets; she broadcasted them from yards away, the way some women telegraphed their approach with perfume. "Yesterday you said, and I quote, 'I have a date with Roger from op-ed tonight, and I'm going to do it with him.'"

Anita collapsed into the chair across from Josie's desk and pouted. "Well, that doesn't mean it was going to happen for sure."

Josie just gave her a give-me-a-break stare. Anita's love life made rabbits look like monks.

"*Once* it didn't happen for sure. . . ." Anita said with a pout.

Josie was saved from hearing further details of the evening by the entrance of her boss, Gus Strauss, a guy in his late thirties who might be almost cute if he'd clean up a little and buy some better ties. He tossed a messy stack of rumpled typed pages onto her desk. "Computer's down. Septuplets story. I need it back by five. Hopefully the copy's not a mess."

Doesn't anyone say hello anymore? Josie wondered. "It is hoped that it's not a mess," she said.

"Huh?" Gus just looked at her.

Josie sighed. How could these people claim to be writers when they were so clueless about using the language properly? "*Hopefully* is an adverb," she explained patiently for the millionth time—knowing it wouldn't be the last. "It means 'with hope.' In your sentence you have it describing the copy, and I'm pretty sure the copy doesn't have any feelings."

Gus and Anita just stared at Josie.

"Well, excuse me for caring about words!" Josie said defensively. She shuffled Gus's pages of copy into one neat stack.

Gus took a moment to turn his flinty-eyed newsman's gaze on Anita. "So. You and Roger in op-ed . . . "

Anita jumped to her feet. "Oh, man! Who told?"

Gus shrugged, as if it should have been obvious. "Roger in op-ed." Then he growled, "Don't make me send you another memo about my policy on interoffice dating."

"*Intra*office," Josie pointed out. "And they're not dating. They're just having—"

"And what is your policy?" Anita shot back. "That if *you're* not getting any, no one can?" She flounced out of the office before he could respond.

"How many times have I fired her?" Gus mumbled.

Josie couldn't keep track. "Five . . . ?" she guessed. "Six . . ."

Gus sighed dramatically and headed for the door.

Stop him! she told herself. *Don't let him leave without asking!*

"Uh, hey, Gus!" she blurted out. "Did you see the story idea I left on your desk?"

"Yeah—the blind foster-home mother." He smiled at her. "It was good."

Josie smiled back. Dare she hope . . . ?

"I got Cahoon on it."

"Oh, Cahoon. Yeah, he's . . . good."

Gus heard the disappointment in her voice and hated it. But what he hated even worse was seeing someone who was damn good at her job mooning over another job that he knew she'd be lousy at. "Geller, we've been over this. You're a great copy editor. Maybe my *best* copy editor. You're not a reporter."

"You've done a lot of my ideas," she pointed out.

Gus acknowledged that with a nod, but said, "You know what separates us office flunkies from the reporters?"

"They don't have to be in the office Christmas show?" she guessed.

Gus shook his head. "A flak jacket."

"A . . . flak jacket."

"Every Tom, Dick, and Harry thinks he can write," Gus said. "But a journalist gets in there, right where the bombs are. He's aggressive. Grabs the bull by the balls."

"You don't think I can grab a bull's balls?" Josie said.

"Geller, you don't want a reporter's life," he promised her. "They're very . . . messy. You're about order. Control. *And* getting me my copy by five."

"Hey—I can be out of control," she shot back.

Gus just smiled and shook his head. On his way out he gave Josie's nameplate a little tap so that it hung at an angle. Then he casually strolled away.

Josie waited. Tormented. But at last she couldn't take it anymore. She dashed to the door and straightened her nameplate again.

A chuckle down the hall told her Gus had been yanking her chain. "Copy by five!" he called.

Josie and Anita met for lunch at the regular place: the cramped, grungy lunchroom in the *Sun-Times* kitchen, down the hall from her office. It didn't have a very high rating—from the food critics or the Health Department—but they were always guaranteed a seat. And you couldn't beat the prices.

Anita was scarfing down some spicy take-out Chinese.

Josie pulled three reclosable plastic bags out of her insulated lunch bag and laid them out on the table. Her lunch was neatly chopped and arranged by category. "Be honest," she asked, as she un-Ziploc'ed her carrot sticks. "Do you think I'm aggressive?"

Anita took a swig of diet cola and considered the question for a moment. "Okay. Remember when they took your office chair in for repairs and forgot to return it?"

"Yeah?"

"You stood for, like, a month."

"So is that a yes or a no?"

A coworker named Cynthia came in and crammed three frozen meals into the food-splattered microwave. She beeped in the programmed cooking time, then dug around in the refrigerator for her soda.

"Just because I'm not out of control doesn't mean I can't write," Josie insisted.

"Josie, you listen to me," Cynthia said. "If you feel you're a writer"—she touched her fingers to her chest—"here, deep inside, don't let anyone tell you you're not. Look at me. Every day I come to this paper and I pour my heart and my soul into what I do. I feel it, passionately, to the core of my being."

"You write obituaries."

"Hey, if you can make a busted aorta sound good—honey, that's art."

The microwave dinged. Cynthia pulled out the three nuked entrees and sat down at the table. Josie glanced around to see who else might be joining them, but for now they appeared to have the small room to themselves. She watched as Cynthia peeled back the film on all three gourmet diet meals, then took a sample bite from each one.

Anita and Josie shared a look.

"Cynthia," Anita said, "aren't they only dietetic if you eat them one at a time?"

Cynthia didn't blink—or stop eating. "I eat 'em one at a time."

Anita let it go and turned back to Josie. "It wouldn't kill you to relax and have some fun. Roger's got a friend, Marshall in editing? Maybe we could double-date."

"Marshall?" Josie exclaimed in disbelief. "You mean 'the Duke'?"

"I swear to God, Jos," Anita said in frustration. "When is the last time you went on a real-live date?"

"I'm concentrating on my career," Josie explained lamely.

Anita jammed her chopsticks into the dregs of her Chinese and leaned forward across the table. "Do you own any colored underwear?" Anita demanded, just as a male coworker entered the room. "Stripes? Anything?"

"Anita!" Josie hissed, embarrassed.

"Look," Anita said with a shrug. "You're way under thirty, you're cute, some guys find white Carter's underwear sexy, but—"

The lone male in the room turned and grinned at them. He was dressed Western-style from head to toe: big bolo tie, silver Texas-size belt buckle, stovepipe jeans, and high-heeled cowboy boots. He pulled a banana out of his rumpled paper lunch bag and performed an elaborate six-shooter routine that would have made Jesse James tremble. Or bust a gut laughing.

The women at the table—all of whom had seen their share of weird guys—managed weak smiles.

"Hi, Marshall," Anita said.

Marshall, playing the strong silent type, exited the lunchroom as if he were John Wayne strolling out of a saloon.

Josie rolled her eyes at Anita. This was her idea of a hot date?

"We could all go line dancing at the Hoof 'n' Foot," Anita suggested dryly.

Josie bit into a carrot stick and stared dreamily out the small smudged window overlooking the street. "The right guy is out there," she said confidently. "I'm just not going to kiss a whole bunch of losers to get to him."

"Yeah, but sometimes kissing the losers can be a fun diversion," Anita pointed out.

"When I finally get kissed, I'll know."

Cynthia nearly choked on her Lean Cuisine. She and Anita shared a look of total disbelief.

"Okay," Anita managed to say at last. "If you've never kissed a guy, we got bigger problems here than underwear."

"I've kissed guys," Josie said defensively. "I've just never *kissed* a guy. Felt that thing—"

"'That thing'?" Cynthia hooted. "Is that what you kids are calling it these days?"

Josie blushed and shook her head. How could she explain to them what she meant? "That thing. That moment. You kiss someone, and it's like the world around you gets all hazy and the only thing in focus is you and this other person, and you know that one person is the person you're meant to be kissing the rest of your life. And for that one moment you've been given this amazing gift and you want to laugh and cry at the same time because you're so lucky you found it and so scared that it will all go away."

Anita and Cynthia stared at Josie, their mouths hanging open.

"Damn, girl!" Cynthia squealed. "You *are* a writer."

Josie spent the evening in her neat, quiet, book-lined apartment stitching LOVE—in cursive letters—into a needlepoint pillow. Much more entertaining than doing the horizontal hoedown with Marshall from editing.

"There. What do you think, guys?" Josie asked. She held her needlework up for her companions to see.

The two turtles in her aquarium nodded.

"Now, where should it go?" Josie looked around the living room, searching for the perfect spot. The pillow had taken many long evenings to complete, so not just anywhere would do. "Hmm . . . "

She cocked her head, pretending to listen to the turtles' advice. "What's that? Bedroom? Great idea!"

Josie clutched the pillow to her heart and carried it into her neat, quiet, book-lined bedroom. The room was pretty, with Laura Ashley prints and ruffles on the bed, chair, and windows. She knew just where to put the pillow, too: propped at the head of her bed—along with the dozen or so other needlepoint pillows she'd completed over the past year.

A girl needed a hobby after all.

"Perfect!" she said, pleased. Her bedroom was lovely, as pretty and tidy as a display in a home-furnishings store. The kind nobody really used.

The editorial staff meeting that would change Josie's life forever took place innocently enough in the *Sun-Times* conference room the following morning.

The day had started out normally for Josie. No important messages. Pencils sharpened and lined up just so. Some rush copy from Gus that *hopefully* wasn't in too bad a shape. Details about Anita's latest *escapades d'amour*.

Then at the appointed hour she'd gotten up and joined the other staffers pouring down the hall into the conference room. *Like cattle stamping to the slaughterhouse*, she always thought. Which in this office wasn't too far from the truth.

She managed to grab a spot at the table next to Anita, then waited nervously with the others to see what Hyram Rigfort, the newspaper's sixty-five-year-old owner, would hurl at them today. Figuratively or literally.

Rigfort sat at the head of the table and smiled at his staff, his perfectly trimmed white hair making him the picture of dignity. He spoke with godlike authority and certitude. "Let me start out by saying that I was very impressed by the investigative piece Dutton did on pesticides in our supermarkets."

Surprised, Dutton sat up straight and smiled proudly. Praise from Rigfort was rare.

"*But*," Rigfort added dramatically, "since the *Trib* did a *better* piece on the *same* subject—you're *fired*."

A choking sound escaped from Dutton's mouth. Everyone else in the room looked horrified. But no one said a word in his defense. No one made a sound of protest. No one wanted to be noticed next. Josie wondered if she could will herself invisible.

"You heard me," Rigfort barked to Dutton. He made a little sweeping motion with his hand across the polished tabletop. "Out. *Out!*"

Now? This instant? Josie gulped. When Rigfort fired you, he didn't fool around.

She felt sorry for Dutton as he dragged himself to his feet, shuffled his papers together, and slunk from the room like a kicked mutt. At least an abandoned dog could count on the ASPCA.

Nervous, Josie plucked a doughnut from the pile in front of her and stuffed it into her mouth.

Rigfort waited until the door clicked closed behind the ex-reporter and then smiled broadly at his remaining staff. "So, Happy March, everybody!

"Happy March, Mister Rigfort," the staff responded in unison, like a class of obedient but miserable schoolkids.

"To celebrate," Rigfort went on, apparently oblivious to the lack of enthusiasm in the room, "I've decided it's time for another undercover piece."

The staff suppressed a groan.

"You all know that some of my best inspirations come from my personal experience," Rigfort said. "Who knew that my botched foray into hair plugs would lead to last month's award-winning exposé—'Hair Today, Gone Tomorrow'? Hats off to you, Bruns."

Bruns, his hair missing in odd-looking clumps, raised a hand in acknowledgment.

"Or should I say 'hats on'?" Rigfort laughed alone at his own joke, then went on. "And what about when my wife had that affair with Gil, her ski instructor, and Henson went undercover as an expert slalom skier?"

Henson smiled but didn't wave. He couldn't—both arms were in casts, souvenirs from the experience.

"So last night I'm sitting around the dinner table with my family," Rigfort continued. "The wife, the two nannies, the boys, and we're eating chicken with this peanut sauce."

"Undercover chef," Gus said. "I like it."

Rigfort shook his head. "Hang on, Gus. So we're eating this peanut sauce and suddenly the younger kid starts choking."

"I'm smelling undercover ER nurse," Anita whispered to Josie.

But the wheels in Rigfort's head were spinning much faster than that.

"Turns out he's allergic to peanuts!" Rigfort exclaimed. "And I think—holy shit! I don't even know my own kids. I mean, who knows if they're even mine? And it got me thinking. How much do we really know about the kids today? What are they thinking? How many of them are allergic to peanuts?"

He scanned the room, his gaze demanding assent and approval. The staff dutifully nodded, totally lost.

Rigfort pounded the table. Josie jumped. "Boom. It hit me—'My Semester in High School.'"

Dead silence.

"You!" Rigfort jabbed a finger. "What's your name?"

Josie blinked. *Me? He's pointing at me?*

Anita jabbed her in the ribs to start her breathing again.

"Josie," she managed. "Josie Geller."

Rigfort nodded. "You enroll on Friday."

The room erupted into general confusion. Josie felt as if she'd been hit by a newspaper-delivery truck.

At last she found her voice. "Oh. But—I'm not a reporter yet—"

"And none of these geezers could pass for a day under forty." Rigfort stood up. As far as he was concerned, everything was decided. "Have fun."

And then he was gone.

Josie floated down the hall to her office. The moment she'd dreamed of . . . It was so unreal, so . . . wonderful! So—her stomach churned—scary.

"It's finally happening, Anita!" she gasped, barely able to speak, she was so excited. She ran both hands through her neatly pulled-back, long, brown hair. "I'm going to *write*." She flung herself into her office chair and planted her hands on her desk. She imagined the pages lying there, no longer someone else's writing for her to clean up like a lowly scullery maid. But *her* story. Her words. Her ideas. "My own undercover feature," she whispered reverently. "'Written by Josie Geller.'" She closed her eyes, afraid she might faint with ecstasy.

"Jos . . ." Anita said.

Josie opened her eyes at the tone in her friend's voice.

"Maybe . . ." Anita bit her lip. "Maybe you should turn it down."

"What?" Josie searched her friend's face—and her heart sank. "You don't think I can do it."

"No," Anita protested. "It's not that. It's just . . . a lot of pressure for your first piece, that's all. I mean, it's not a half-page article, it's a major undercover piece. Look what Rigfort did to Dutton—and that guy's his cousin!"

Gus rushed in then and shut the door. He leaned over Josie's desk and reassured her, "Don't worry, I'll straighten all this out."

Gus, too? Josie sighed. Not the vote of confidence she would have wanted. "But I don't want it straightened out," Josie said.

"Geller, this one is way out of your league."

Josie sat back in her chair and glared at her so-called friends. "Okay, just so I'm clear here—neither of you thinks I can do this."

"Jos," Anita said gently, "that's not what we're—"

"Anita," Josie interrupted, angry, "when you wanted to seduce that guy in the mailroom and you didn't think you could learn Spanish fast enough, who quizzed you on your verbs?"

Anita looked down. "Señorita Josie."

"And Gus—when you picked up knitting, who showed you how to hold the needles?"

Gus's cheeks reddened. "You did," he admitted quietly.

"You *knit*?" Anita asked, surprised.

Gus shrugged.

"So," Josie said. "this is my chance."

Gus stuffed his hands in his pockets and stared at the floor. He'd been filled with dreams like that once. And it had been a long time since he'd seen such eagerness in the eyes of a reporter.

What the hell. "I'm not holding your job for you, Geller," he grumbled.

With a squeal, Josie jumped up and hugged her boss.

The old grouch squirmed, uncomfortable with the display of affection. "Don't make me send you the memo on hugging in the workplace."

Josie just smiled as she watched her boss hurry out to hide his blush.

Then she felt Anita's hand on her arm. "I do believe in you, Jos. Anything you need, I'll help you out."

Josie sank into her chair and motioned to the brown paper bag neatly tucked between her dictionary and her thesaurus. "You could start by handing me that bag."

Puzzled, Anita removed the bag and handed it to her friend.

Josie stuck it over her face, flipped her head between her knees, and started breathing frantically into the bag. Okay, so she was hyperventilating.

Her friends were behind her. They believed in her.

Did she believe in herself?

3

Josie needed a car.

She had a feeling her conservative mid-sized Buick wouldn't cut it with the high-school crowd. She needed undercover wheels, a car that wouldn't scream "responsible adult" every time she pulled into the parking lot. And she knew exactly where to find it.

From her brother, Rob, who, despite being twenty-three, had yet to exhibit any of the qualities that would have identified him as a responsible adult. He still lived at home with their mom and dad, for example. And for a career choice? He was employed at the Tiki Post, a mailbox and copy shop with a Tahitian theme. Josie suspected the only reason he chose this job over a post at

McDonald's or the quick mart was the uniform: flip-flops and a Hawaiian shirt.

And what kind of car could you afford on a Tiki Post salary? A rusting yellow Vega that—like disco—had seen better days.

Rob shook his head. "No. Uh-uh."

"Please, Rob," she begged. They were standing outside the Tiki Post, where she'd parked her car behind his.

"Why don't you borrow Mom's car?"

"I can't use a new *minivan*! I need a cheap car"—she caught herself, editing her words in midsentence—"a vintage classic. It's just for a couple of months."

Rob lovingly stroked a dented fender. "A couple of months is like ten years in Bambi's life."

"That is so *weird* that you named your car," she told him.

"Hey, guys name their—"

"Okaaaay, let's not go there." She took a deep breath and, before she had time to change her mind, quickly said, "I'll give you my Buick Le Sabre."

Rob hooted with laughter and disappeared into the store.

Hey, what's wrong with my car?

"You can name it whatever you want!" Josie shouted after him. She ran to the store entrance and yanked open the door—which triggered an automatic blast of Hawaiian music. Monty Maylik, the fiftyish owner of the place, stepped forward to greet her by slipping a plastic hot-pink lei over her head. "Aloha! Welcome!" he said cheerfully.

"Relax, Monty," Rob said. "It's just my sister."

Monty's smile melted like ice cubes on Waikiki. He yanked the "free" lei from around her neck and disappeared behind the counter.

Josie shook her head as she looked around the store. Her brother was a smart guy; she couldn't believe he'd allowed himself to wind up in this dead-end job. Just look. Monty was practicing chords on his ukulele. Rob was arranging a display of envelopes. Josie shivered. It was such a waste! "Did you call that admissions lady at Lakeshore Community College?"

"No."

"She can still get you in for the fall semester, maybe even get you a baseball scholarship . . . "

"I'm not going to college, Jos," Rob snapped. "And I'm not playing any more baseball." He gestured at the store around him. "This is my life."

"This?" Josie exclaimed. She glanced at Monty and lowered her voice. "This is a luau that sells packing material," she whispered. "You had a real shot at playing college ball, and you let one case of mono stop everything. Don't you want more? To move out of Mom and Dad's? Pay your own bills?"

"So I can be as happy as you?" he shot back.

Ouch. The barb hurt. But today Josie had something to shoot back with. "For your information," she announced proudly, "you're looking at the newest *Sun-Times* undercover reporter. Starting Friday, I'm Josie Geller, high-school senior. Class of 1999."

Rob's reaction wasn't quite the one she'd been hoping for. He started laughing.

"What?"

Rob could hardly control himself. "Do you remember high school?"

She lowered her eyes. "It was a long time ago—"

"Don't you remember what they called you?"

Don't think about it, she told herself. *It's over. It's in the past. It doesn't matter anymore. . . . Stop!*

But she couldn't stop. The memory engulfed her like a merciless tidal wave. . . .

The cafeteria is packed with kids. Everyone's chanting, as if it were a pep rally. Except the only sport here is to humiliate the geek: "Josie Grossie, Josie Grossie, Josie Grossie . . . "

Josie looked stricken. Her own lips betrayed her by speaking the dreaded words aloud: "Josie Grossie."

"I know." Rob peered at his sister. "You look nauseous."

Josie swayed on her feet, her hands clutching her

stomach. "Nauseated," she whispered. *Nauseous* meant "causing nausea or disgust." *Nauseated* meant "sick to her stomach, about to throw up." Which she was about to do.

"Oh, God." She covered her mouth with her hand and raced for the rest room, where her body did its best to rid her of the horrible memory.

When the attack was over, she slowly rose from her knees and tore off a neat section of toilet paper to wipe her mouth. But when she looked down at her feet . . .

She's wearing brown-leather oxfords. Nerdy brown-leather oxfords. Braces. And heavy glasses. She is walking down the hall, minding her own business.

A boy sneaks up behind her and carefully peels back the top of her backpack while another boy pours in half a can of Sprite.

Josie continues down the hall as the Sprite seeps into her pack, around her books, gravity dragging it down in a search for an outlet.

She stops when she reaches Billy Prince, ultimate high-school heartthrob. She has decided she can't go another day without speaking to him. She's practiced what to say over and over. Now she approaches him nervously.

"Hey, Billy Prince," she begins as the Sprite accumulates in the bottom of her pack. "I noticed you weren't in math today, and I have the notes in case you want—"

Josie freezes when she hears an odd sound.

The sound of liquid hitting linoleum.

She follows Billy's surprised gaze down to the sound—beneath her pleated skirt, between her nerdy oxfords.

Sprite—pooling between her feet like pee.

For three seconds—or three eternities, Josie isn't sure which—the hall falls silent. Except for the sound of a seventeen-year-old girl peeing on the floor.

And then Billy throws back his head and laughs, the sound bouncing off the metal lockers, telegraphing everyone within hearing distance that it's cool to join him in laughing at this pitiful excuse for a girl. . . .

Josie gripped the edge of the small, grungy, porcelain sink and stared at her face in the mirror. She was twenty-five years old, a responsible adult, with an apartment and a job at a major newspaper, and she was standing in the rest room of the Tiki Post, a cheesy strip-mall store where her infuriating brother worked.

But all she could see staring back at her from the mirror was the seventeen-year-old Josie. Glasses, braces, dorky hair. Total geek. Total misfit. Total loser.

She'd been so god-awful grateful to finally graduate out of that hellhole known as high school.

And now she was going back. On purpose.

4

"So you were a geek. Big deal."

Josie and Anita were at the mall, browsing through a Teen Clothing Store—Josie wasn't sure now which one without going back outside to check the sign; inside they all looked alike to her. The walls were plastered with giant blowups showing utterly happy gorgeous guys and girls in suggestive poses, dressed in extremely overpriced clothes that looked to Josie as if they'd been dug out of the bargain barrel at the thrift shop.

Shopping here was like trying to read Italian—she didn't have the vocabulary. Except for some basic shapes she recognized, it was all gibberish.

Josie picked up a huge platform shoe. *My God, it must weigh five pounds!* she thought. Wearing two would easily replace a workout at the gym. "Remember espadrilles?" she asked Anita.

"Please. That doesn't make you a nerd. Everyone wore those shoes."

Josie shook her head. "The girls *threw* them at me in the locker room."

Anita cleared her throat. "Okaaay. That's bad," she admitted.

"At the end of the year the person who got the most direct hits to my head got to toss me into the pool."

"*Mama mia!*" Anita held a hand to her chest and took a deep breath, trying to recover from the utter horror of the story. When she'd recovered, she searched for something positive to say. "Just because you were a nerd once doesn't mean it's going to happen again." She squeezed Josie's hand and grinned. "That's why you have me for fashion consultation."

She flicked through the rack, eyeing the garments quickly and critically, then pulled a slip skirt off the rack and held it up. "Now this is cute."

A blush crept over Josie's cheek. "*That* is lingerie," she replied.

Reluctantly Anita jammed it back on the rack and kept looking. There were tons of things here that she'd wear in a minute, but for Josie . . . well, they'd have to find something just right. "So I was thinking about what you were saying—you know, about really being kissed?"

Josie nodded.

Anita hunched her shoulders and grinned like a little girl. "I think Roger could be the one."

"What did you feel when you kissed him?" Josie asked eagerly.

Anita stroked a black stretch-velvet T and thought back to the experience. "Bridgework?"

Josie rolled her eyes and crossed to another rack. Then her eyes lit up, and she pulled out a plain brown cardigan. "How about this?"

Anita looked stricken and said in her best motherly voice, "I am *not* letting you out of the house in *that*, young lady!" Worried, she glanced around the store, then pounced. In her hands: a white marabou jacket and matching earrings. "Cuuuute!"

Marabou, Josie thought. *Any of several large African storks or a hat or garment trimmed with the down from the underside of such a stork.* She'd had to look that up once when fact-checking an article for the paper.

Yeah, right. She'd look like Big Bird's cousin in that.

"Anita," she reminded her friend, "this is about reporting, not accessorizing."

Anita held the jacket up in front of Josie. She eyed her critically and began plucking at strands of her limp brown hair. "And we're going to have to do *something* about your hair."

"Anita!"

"Jos, please try and have some fun here, okay? How many of us get to go back to high school?" She gave her friend a quick squeeze, then dragged her toward the dressing room. "You're gonna have a *blast*!"

Maybe, Josie thought, eyeing the horrible marabou with trepidation. To her it seemed like an omen.

When the alarm rang the next morning, Josie sat up in bed and shrieked at the reflection in the mirror of her dressing table.

There was a blonde in her bed!

She yanked the covers up around her and glanced around.

She was—as always—alone.

Her hand shot to her hair, and she laughed.

She'd forgotten she'd trimmed and dyed her hair—Anita had insisted. The remnants of their marathon makeover session were scattered across her bedside table and floor: makeup tubes, hair-color boxes, cover-up pencils, white lipstick, red lipstick—green lipstick. And then there was her research. Pages ripped from *Seventeen*, *YM*, and other teen magazines demonstrating not only how she was supposed to dress, but also how she was supposed to stand, sit, look, laugh, frown, pout, glare.

Josie jumped out of bed and flipped on the radio. The familiar voices of National Public Radio greeted her. She knew she probably should tune in to a more youthful station that might help her get into character for her big undercover mission. But she was a journalist—she couldn't start the day without her NPR news fix.

Josie flung herself into the shower, washed her hair, and then sat down at her dressing table. The face staring back at her looked terrified. For a moment she thought about calling in sick.

But she couldn't do that. This was her big chance. Her chance to write. Her chance to prove to everyone at the paper that there was more to her than dangling participles and split infinitives.

And maybe, too, to show Billy Prince and everyone who'd ever called her Josie Grossie that she was special.

With determination she snatched up an eye crayon and began to draw on a seventeen-year-old face.

First day of high school. Hey, she'd already done it once before. Ought to be a piece of cake.

Half an hour later Josie switched on the ignition in the old yellow Vega. Rob had finally relented and switched cars with her, but as she jolted into the morning rush-hour traffic she wondered if Bambi's backfiring was a protest to having strange hands on the steering wheel. After a short drive listening to the NPR news update, she saw it up ahead. Her destination.

Southglen South High School.

It was a typical suburban high-school campus anchored by a main building and surrounded by tasteful trees and landscaping. A solid, sensible building conducive to the education of Chicago's youth.

Josie drove into the parking lot, circled until she found a tight spot she could squeeze into. She cut the ignition, and Bambi backfired once more, just to have the final word.

Josie glanced out the window and saw a whole parking lot full of cool kids freeze, staring at her as if she were a what's-wrong-with-this-picture? puzzle. The next moment they dismissed her as if she no longer existed.

She remembered that feeling.

Josie gripped the steering wheel and took a few deep breaths to stave off the sudden wave of terror that threatened to send her fleeing. "Okay, I can do this. Piece of cake. I can do this."

After all, I'm a grown-up, she told herself. *I have an apartment. A job. I pay bills.*

These other kids are just . . . kids!

Chin up, attitude adjusted, she stepped out of the car, confident in her new teen clothes: the marabou jacket and earrings over tight white jeans. *Looking good, feeling good,* she told herself. *You go, girl!*

Do they still say that?

She slammed the car door behind her and strode toward school with confidence . . .

Not seeing that she'd slammed the car door on her jacket. Not hearing a piece of marabou rip as she walked away. Not knowing it trailed behind her like a long feathery tail.

Thinking only, *Yeah, okay. Feeling good . . .*

She strode toward the school as if she knew where she was going, walked up the steps and through those gaping doors as if she'd been there a thousand times. As if she owned the place.

But then she found herself swallowed up like a spit in the ocean, when a wave of kids swept her up and carried her toward the lobby. Jostling along, she studied her surroundings, overwhelmed by the noise—it seemed as if everyone was talking at once. A huge banner that shouted GO RAMS! 63 DAYS TILL PROM reminded her of what was important here.

When at last she again felt under the power of her own two feet, she plastered herself up against the wall and surreptitiously pulled out her stack of note cards. "My name is Josie," she muttered, rehearsing her lines. "I'm from Scranton, Pennsylvania. Our state bird is the ruffed grouse. . . ." She figured a girl from Pennsylvania would know such things about her state, right? "Our main exports are steel, chocolate, and the Amish. . . . My favorite Spice Girl is Posh. . . ." Hmm, were the Spice Girls still hip? Maybe she shouldn't mention something as ephemeral as favorite celebrities—at least not until she got her feet wet and got a feel for what was popular at Southglen South. Checking her watch, she stuffed the cards back into her purse and began to inch her way along the wall.

She was surprised at how nervous she was. Would the other students be able to tell at a glance that she had aged out of high school all of seven years ago? Twenty-five had seemed ancient when she was in high school. She felt like a spy. No one here—not even the principal—had any idea she wasn't legit. She wondered briefly if impersonating a high-school student was illegal in Illinois. Surely Mr. Rigfort wouldn't ask her to do something that was against the law, would he?

Don't answer that, she told herself. Rigfort struck her as the kind of man who made up his own rules. *Just keep your head down and act as if you belong here.*

She nearly shrieked when a guard grabbed her arm.

"Hey—where you going?"

Josie gulped as she stared up into his stern face. Caught already?

"Oh, I'm a student. Most definitely a student. In high school. Here." She pointed firmly at the floor. "I am going to class. With my fellow students." She smiled blindly into the river of kids, tossing perky little waves at random passersby. "Hi. Hi there! Hel-loo!"

The guard just stared at her, his face as friendly as a brick wall at the end of an alley. Then he motioned behind them.

She turned around. *Whoa!* Now she understood. All the students were being herded through three absolutely huge metal detectors. Josie shuddered. Had they had trouble of some kind here? Things had changed a *lot* since she went to high school.

She smiled at the guard. "Whoops!" Then she walked back to go through with the others.

"Freak," the guard muttered under his breath.

Josie faced the metal detectors with an overwhelming sense of dread—and not just because she always felt creepy around them. Today she was toting some major bell ringers. On the outside her backpack looked like any ordinary kid's backpack—giant, but ordinary. But inside she'd hidden the various electronic tools of the investigative-reporter trade that might blow her cover if revealed.

A film of perspiration broke out on her upper lip; her armpits felt damp beneath the marabou jacket. She felt like a spy from a Cold War suspense film and knew that what happened as she stepped through these electronic portals could make or break her mission in an instant.

Crossing her fingers, trying to look nonchalant and cool, she stepped through.

She jumped at the alarm.

Ohgodohgodohgodohgod.

Now the sweat was a river navigating her spine. *I'll never get out of this alive,* she told herself. *I'll humiliate myself. I'll lose my job. I won't be able to pay my rent, and I'll wind up on a park bench somewhere wearing a smelly old dress and doing lunch with the pigeons. . . .*

With her eyes on the toes of her shoes, she stepped up to the long post-metal-detector spill-your-guts-to-the-world table and heaved her heavy backpack from her shoulder. She tried to act casual as the guard unzipped the pack with crisp motions and dumped the contents out for everyone and his sister to see.

Cell phone. Laptop. Mini tape recorder. Electronic organizer. Pager.

The guard scrutinized the pile, and Josie felt her heart skip a beat, then pound in terror. Adrenaline pumped through her veins. The fight-or-flight response—her body urging her either to punch somebody in the nose or flee and forget the whole thing. But as a civilized adult she could do neither. She had to stand and take whatever they dished out. She could feel the eyes of every student and faculty member in the school boring so many holes into her back she'd end up looking like Swiss cheese.

The guard's hand shot out—

Oh, God!

And picked up one small item.

It flashed menacingly in the morning light shining in through the window.

A thin metal nail file.

"Weapon," the guard barked with disgust, then pointedly tossed it in the trash.

Josie blinked, trying to force her heart—and her breakfast—back down to their proper locations in her body. That was it? He was more concerned about a nail file than all her high-tech spy equipment? He wasn't calling out the dogs or, even worse, the principal?

Without moving her head, she glanced down the table at the other piles of student belongings—and nearly laughed out loud.

They all had identical piles of high-tech equipment.

High school. At least when it came to possessions, things had definitely changed.

• • •

Josie seemed to be the only thing in the halls that wasn't moving. Trying not to get run over, she stared at her class schedule, then up at the seemingly endless doors opening off the hall. *Just ask,* she told herself. *Don't be shy. You belong here, remember?*

Scanning the crowd, she located a guy who seemed fairly normal and approached him for directions. "Hi—um, I'm looking for Room 204, Ms. Knox?"

As the boy pointed down the hall and began to speak, something shiny caught Josie's eyes. Something inside the guy's mouth.

"Take a right at Miss Arnasall's room, then at the bathroom . . . "

It was a tiny silver ball in the center of his tongue.

". . . go down the stairs, left at the admin office . . . "

Oh. My. God. His tongue is pierced!

". . . right at the prom banner—204 is across the hall."

Josie was mesmerized, unable to tear her eyes from the metal slicing through flesh, her face contorted into an expression of pain. "Ow."

The boy looked at her as if she were insane.

"I—I mean, wow. Wow! Great directions." She nodded, forcing her gaze away from his mouth, upward, to his now-contemptuous eyes. "Clear. Concise."

Hoisting her backpack higher on her shoulder, she stumbled off, totally embarrassed. Her brain hadn't absorbed a single word of his directions.

And behind her—did she imagine it?—a single uttered oath:

"Freak."

The bell had rung by the time Josie figured out how to get to Room 204 by herself. She peeked in through the doorway, hoping for a kind soul at the front of the room. Ms. Knox, mid-forties, with a bubbly smile, looked promising.

"Hi—hello," the teacher called out. "*Wilkommen. Entrez.*"

This was not the way Josie had wanted to start her day. She'd hoped to slip into the classroom unnoticed and hole up at the back of the room, where she could conduct her research on teenagers in high school without being scrutinized herself.

Instead, she was being stared at like a bug under a microscope. *Or maybe a germ*, she thought, given the way some of the kids were looking at her. At least the teacher seemed nice. Ducking her head, Josie hesitantly walked into the room. "Sorry I'm late."

Somebody in the back of the room snickered.

"Yes, well, I'm sorry I forgot to take my hot-flash medication this morning," Ms. Knox quipped. She glanced down at her class list. "Josie, right?"

Josie nodded.

"Please, sit." She waved her pudgy arm toward a seat on the far side of the room. "*Mi casa es su casa.*"

Josie felt every eye in the room devouring her as she made her way across the front of the class, still unaware that she was trailing a marabou tail. She awkwardly maneuvered her way down the aisle to her seat, trying not to trip over outstretched feet or bump anybody with her overloaded backpack. She pretended not to hear the snickers rippling across the room. She took her seat, unable not to notice the two totally intimidating model-beautiful girls sitting directly behind her.

"That is so sad. . . ." one said, not bothering to whisper.

"I know," her friend replied. "Like five chickens had to die just so she could look that stupid."

Josie fought the blush that rose up her neck like the mercury on a hot day. She wrestled it, tried to swallow it, tried to use mental-imagery techniques to pound it back down with a hammer, tried hypnotizing herself out of it, tried a prayer . . .

But ultimately the blush would have its way, and she felt its heat flush across her pale cheeks—a red flag announcing to the world that the girls' cruel remarks had cut her to the quick—and had mattered.

Too bad she and Anita had wasted so much money on that department store blush.

Keep your eye on your goal, Josie, she reminded herself. And she did her best to bear it.

"Josie," Ms. Knox said in a cheerful voice that belied the words to follow, "in my class tardiness is unacceptable—"

The class began to laugh, as if they knew what was coming.

Josie squirmed. "I'm *really* sorry—"

"Not as sorry as I am." Ms. Knox reached beneath her desk and pulled out a sombrero. A ridiculously *huge* sombrero. Something that would be totally humiliating to—

Ms. Knox ceremoniously placed it on Josie's head.

—wear.

"Olé!" Ms. Knox giggled. "Ten minutes in this hat, you'll never be late again. So, let's hear something about you. Stand up. Stand up."

Josie couldn't believe it. Not only did she have to wear this ridiculous hat, she had to stand up in front of the class while wearing it?

With great effort she stood up, and the sombrero drooped over her eyes. More snickers. She would have been glad to remain hidden beneath the hat's droopy brim, but she forced herself to shove it up enough for her to glance at her note cards. She skimmed the one that was neatly headed MY PAST, then laid the cards facedown on her desk. "My name is Josie. I'm a high-school student. I came from—"

The classroom door swung open, and Josie looked up. And in the blinding light from the hallway, she squinted in disbelief as a shadowy vision of Billy Prince emerged from the light.

"Billy?" Josie whispered.

But then she blinked, and she realized that it wasn't—of course, could never have been—Billy Prince, but another just as totally beautiful guy.

"B-Bali," Josie stammered, trying to cover her mistake. "I'm from . . . Billy-Bali. It's a suburb of Bali proper. . . ."

She trailed off as she watched the beautiful guy toss a wooden hall pass to Ms. Knox, then swing into his seat.

"Bali?" Ms. Knox was saying. "Fascinating! What did your family do there?"

"Uh—" Josie looked around in a panic, and as her eyes fell on a student wearing a Southglen South windbreaker, who turned away momentarily, revealing the huge ram on the back, she heard the word "sheep" roll out of her mouth. "We were . . . sheep . . . farmers. We raised sheep. In Billy-Bali."

Josie closed her eyes, realizing what a total mess she'd just gotten herself into. "Oh, my God," she whispered. Then corrected, "Oh, my God—do I miss Billy-Bali." She bit her lip. "It had—"

What? What did it have, Josie? You've never been to Bali in your life, never even copyedited a travel article about Bali!

"—a . . . really great . . . aquarium."

Josie, listen closely, she told herself. *Shut—your—mouth. And sit down.*

She closed her mouth and sat down, feeling totally defeated. The rest of the class was mostly a blur.

Rushing to her next class, toting her enormous book bag, she ducked her chin and whispered covertly into her handheld tape recorder: "Note to self. Research Bali. Kill Anita for picking this outfit. . . . Find—and destroy—sombrero."

5

Safe!

Josie managed to find her next class on her own and on time—in fact, early enough to grab one of the prized seats at the back of the room. She dropped her backpack to the floor with a thud, took a deep breath, and tried to relax. *I'll be safe here*, she told herself, slouching low into her seat. *Just be quiet and no one will notice you.*

Wrong.

Josie felt the heat of their glare before she looked up and saw them: The two beauties from Ms. Knox's class—whom she'd heard called Kristen and Kirsten—joined now by another of their kind. If looks could kill, she wouldn't even be having this thought right now. She'd be a puddle of ectoplasm shimmering on the institutional tile floor.

They descended upon her like the Three Musketeers from the Gap.

"We sit here," Kristen said.

Don't apologize, Josie! she warned herself. *Stand your ground. Remember those inspiring words from the* Desiderata: *"You are a child of the universe, no less than the trees and the stars; you have a right to be here. . . ." Remember—*

But her traitorous mouth was already chanting the universal mantra of the uncool when in confrontation with the cool: "Um, I'm sorry. . . ."

The apology did not move them.

"I—I didn't know the seats were assigned," she explained.

"They're not," the new girl said.

Josie got the message, and for now—still fragile from the recent humiliation with the sombrero—she chose retreat over a showdown. She quickly gathered her things and moved forward one row, beside two other empty seats.

A sweet smoky aroma announced the next two arrivals. Two stoned-out-looking dudes with shoulder-length hair paused at her desk and stared down in the general direction of her face. "Sorry," one said. "We sit here."

Josie glanced around, then pointed at the two

empty seats. "Couldn't you . . . um, sit there?"

"Right," Stoner Number 2 said sarcastically. He put one hand on his hip. "Except, like, there are *three* of us . . . ?"

Josie double-checked her math on the situation here. Still looked like just two of them to her. She watched the swaying students slowly count themselves—one . . . two . . . They looked at each other, then the two seats. Back at each other . . .

And then a look of pure unadulterated horror erupted on the first one's face.

"Dude!" he gasped. "We left Jed at the 7-Eleven!" He ran both hands through his long, sun-streaked locks. "Again!"

I think I'll just move, Josie thought, feeling like a bag lady in an unfriendly neighborhood. She gathered her things and dragged them to the very last available seat in the room.

In the front row.

Where only nerds and teachers' pets sit.

But she was out of options, and the final bell was ringing, so she settled herself with plans to make the best of it. She glanced down the row, surreptitiously studying the other students around her.

Hmm, this was new. These front-rowers were all wearing the same thing, which was weird enough. But what the same thing was was orange sweatshirts with the word *Denominator* on them.

Fans of Arnold Schwarzenegger's new action flick? she guessed. Somehow she didn't think so.

She noticed that the girl sitting right next to her was wearing a whole collection of medals pinned to her sweatshirt. And one other unusual thing. A smile.

Josie smiled back. The tension in the back of her neck eased just a little.

Just then a man rushed in to the front of the room, banishing all thoughts of orange sweatshirts from her mind.

He was beautiful.

That was the first thing she noticed about him. But there was more to him than that. There was something in the way he moved, the way he laid his briefcase on the teacher's desk, pulled out books, notebook, pens. He seemed like a person who knew where he belonged—not cocky like the guy in Ms. Knox's class, or aggressive like the Gap triplets. But a confidence that came from self-knowledge. He seemed like a man who knew his purpose in life. Unlike most of the people Josie saw each day, he looked awake. Alive. Going somewhere.

He then came around to sit casually on the front of the desk. Without speaking a word, he removed the plastic lid from a paper cup of coffee, took a long, luxurious drink, then sighed blissfully—a sound that did funny things to Josie's insides.

Who was this guy? He looked too mature to be a student—she estimated he was about her age or a little older. But he looked too intelligent—and too ruggedly good-looking—to be a teacher. *Guest speaker?* she guessed.

Whoever he was, she hoped he planned to come back again tomorrow, because one day definitely wasn't enough time to admire him completely.

He smiled at the class. "Hi, everyone." Then his eyes fell on Josie, and he smiled at her—a genuine smile that made her feel welcome for the first time that day. "I don't think we've met. I'm Sam Coulson—"

Sam. The name fit him. Straightforward. Honest. Friendly. Inviting. . . .

". . . although for some reason the school has this thing about not letting you guys call me Sam."

She would never be able to call him anything else. . . .

Josie gave herself a mental shake. So he *was* the teacher. And she'd have to call him Mr. Coulson—at least to his face.

"I'm Josie," she said shyly. "Geller. I think the school would probably be comfortable with you calling me that. Josie."

Sam Coulson grinned. "Josie, since you're new—I love to drink my coffee during class, and since I allow myself to do this, I allow everyone to bring beverages to class as well. Welcome to Shakespeare's *As You Like It.*" He looked around hopefully at all his students. "Okay. How many of you actually read the assignment last night?"

About five hands went up.

"Not bad," Mr. Coulson said. "Now, how many of you spent more than thirty minutes eating salty snack foods?"

About twenty hands shot into the air.

Sam laughed and shook his head. "Man. If I could just get you guys to read while you eat." He reached for his textbook and began flipping through the pages.

Josie felt someone nudge her and braced for another insult. But when she looked over she was surprised to see the girl in the orange Denominator sweatshirt holding out her textbook. *My God,* Josie thought. *She's actually offering to share her book.*

Josie mouthed, *Thank you,* and reached out to hold her side of the book. It gave her a peaceful feeling, like sharing a hymnal with her grandma in church when she was little.

"*As You Like It,*" Sam began, "is an example . . . "

As he got up and turned to write on the blackboard, about half the class—all the girls, and one or two of the boys—nearly swooned over the rear view he presented in his 501 jeans.

". . . of a Shakespearean *Pastoral* Comedy," Sam went on, unaware of the stir he was creating. "Anyone know what that means?"

Josie felt a strong urge to answer, but quickly extinguished it. She'd attracted enough attention already today; no sense in actually raising her hand to invite people to stare at her.

"Oh oh oh! That's what they do to milk!" an enthusiastic but clueless girl in the third row blurted out.

"Uh, that's *pasteurize*, Sera," Sam pointed out politely. "But close. Same letter—" He tapped three fingers on his arm, as if playing charades. "Three syllables . . . "

"Parakeet?" Sera tried.

The Denominator girl sitting next to Josie whispered, "There's a minute of my life I'll never get back."

Josie had to duck her head to hide her grin.

"Okay." Sam rubbed his hands over his face, then asked the class, "Anyone else?"

He looked so . . . so needy, Josie thought. And the next thing she knew she was blurting out the answer: "*Pastoral* means set in the country. Originally seen in the *Eclogues of Virgil*. It's from the Latin *pascere*. 'To graze.'"

A student somewhere in the back bleated like a sheep.

Sam just stared at her, smiling in disbelief that such a miracle had occurred in his class. "Are you sure you're seventeen?"

Josie nearly freaked. Had she given herself away? *What were you thinking!* she scolded herself. But then she told herself to calm down. He was only joking. "Oh, definitely. Yup. Seventeen."

Then Sam did something she'd never seen a teacher do: He reached out and shook her hand. "Pleasure having you in the class, Josie Geller." He glanced around the room at the rest of his students, most of whom had lapsed into various stages of distraction, boredom, or sleep. "Did I mention to the class that I love our new student?"

Josie beamed. For the first time that day she felt as if she had a right to her small scrap of personal space.

But then, from the back of the room, she heard Kristen and Kirsten's friend say, "Did I mention that the class also loves our new kiss-ass?"

Josie's joy soured.

"Gibby," Sam said sternly, "that's not exactly the kind of participation I'm looking for."

"Sorry," she said, not sounding it.

Josie hibernated for the rest of the class, despite a few attempts by Mr. Coulson to get her to contribute again. When the bell rang, she fled to her locker, only to find she couldn't get to it because two students were using it to prop themselves up during a marathon make-out session.

Josie waited patiently, hoping they'd finish up before the next bell rang, and she seemed to be the only one listening to the voice of a girl making an announcement on the intercom.

"Hi, this is Sydney, student body president! Okay, first. Bad news—the district didn't allocate enough funds, so as of this afternoon, there will be no music department. Now about the prom—"

Everyone in the entire school seemed to screech to a halt. Even the couple using her locker came up for air long enough to listen.

"Voting on prom theme has been completed," Sydney's voice rang out in the silent halls. "And the theme is—"

The students held their breath.

"The . . . millennium!"

The school erupted into celebration. In the classrooms kids cheered and pounded their desk-tops. In the halls they shouted, clapped, and banged their lockers . . . and one girl even fainted.

Josie made a mental note to add this info to her reporter's notebook: a) Prom is very important at Southglen South and b) the students unanimously approved of the theme.

Then everyone in the crowded hall began moving again, sweeping Josie into an eddy that swirled her toward a locker door that just opened. Josie's face and the metal door collided, and the door won.

What magic is it, thought Josie, as she checked to see if her nose was broken, *that makes sure a clumsy move like that is seen by the most popular hunk in school?* The cool guy from Ms. Knox's class was not only there to see it, but to lead everyone else in the laughter.

Josie glanced at her watch. She felt as if she'd been through at least three days of school. But it was lunchtime. And that could mean only one thing.

The ultimate humiliation.

The cafeteria.

Please, she begged the Fates. *Please don't make me eat at a table all alone. . . .*

Josie chose the top tray and slid it down the aluminum runner bars of the line. It was like a tour of gourmet specialties—on another planet. UFOs. As in Unidentified Food Objects.

And the worst of it? This awful-looking vat of coleslaw.

"Excuse me," Josie found herself asking a guy wearing a plastic cap behind the steaming vats of food. "What's in the coleslaw?"

The cafeteria guy grunted and hauled an industrial-sized plastic tub onto the counter. He turned it so she could read the label: KOLE SLAW FOOD. Josie wrinkled her nose and hurried to the end of the line.

"That'll be twelve ninety-five," the cashier announced.

"Oh, my gosh," Josie said. "That's pricey."

"That's real meat in the ham sandwich," the lady pointed out.

Josie turned to the girl behind her and joked, "Boy—that's a lot of bread for that bread!"

The girl made a face at her lame joke and reached past her for the yellow plastic mustard bottle.

Yellow plastic mustard bottle . . .

Josie stared at it, remembering . . .

She is standing, paralyzed, in the middle of the cafeteria while kids at the tables chant, "Josie Grossie, Josie Grossie . . ." Only later, looking in the mirror in the girls' room, does she see the word "Grossie" tattooed across her back in a cursive ribbon of yellow mustard.

Josie banished the vision with a shake of her head and stared out across the crowded cafeteria, searching for a place to sit.

Kristen, Kirsten, and Gibby sat together, of course. Josie braced herself and headed for their table.

"Kirsten," Kristen said, "that bran muffin has like seventy fat grams."

"Nah-uh."

"Yeah," Gibby insisted. "I read this thing that one bran muffin can be like two bran muffins sometimes."

Kristen shoved the food away as if it were pork rinds. "God. Food can be so confusing."

Josie chose that moment to speak. "Hi, Kristen."

"It's Kirsten," the girl said.

Good move, Josie. She slid into a seat at the end of the table and took a spiral pad out of her backpack. In the process she spilled chocolate milk all over her white jeans.

"That'll teach me to wear white after Labor Day," she said, trying to cover her clumsiness with some humor.

"Um, I don't think you're supposed to wear white jeans after 1983," Gibby commented.

Everyone laughed.

Josie faked a laugh, pretending to be in on the joke, instead of the butt of it. "Right, right." *Hang in there, forge ahead. Think of the writing.* With great effort she picked up her notepad and pen. "So—tell me about yourselves." *Please.*

But they all just stared at her in disgust.

"I'm Guy."

Josie looked up into the eyes of one of the most beautiful guys she'd ever seen this side of the movies. Guy was the guy from Ms. Knox's class. "Yes, you are," she said, flustered. "A guy. Guy. Quite a guy. Oh, my. Look at that—I rhymed." She laughed nervously. "Yikes . . . Bikes!"

"Are you in special ed?" Guy asked seriously.

Mortified, Josie jumped to her feet, grabbed her backpack and pen and notebook—and her chocolate milk. "Bye. Guy. Others." Then she fled toward the door of the cafeteria. "Aaaaah! How old am I?" she exclaimed, as she passed a table surrounded by orange sweatshirts.

One of the Denominators instantly answered, "Approximately six thousand three hundred and fifty days old—subject to adjustment for date of birth."

The rest of the Denominators laughed.

Josie pushed through the cafeteria doors—

Right into a huge wall of a guy with a security uniform on.

"You got a pass?" the guard demanded.

No, Josie thought morosely. *I don't have a pass. I have no business being here at all.*

6

So far Josie's first day back in high school was going normally.

She'd been ridiculed by a teacher, degraded by her fellow students, injured by a locker door, and laughed at in the cafeteria. Could it get any worse?

Yes, it could.

Josie had forgotten about one of the most humiliating experiences in the universe, even worse than sitting alone in the cafeteria, something that could bring a smart, educated girl like herself to her knees begging for mercy.

Gym class.

It was bad enough that they forced you against your will to attempt impossible physical activities that could only make you look foolish. But they also made you wear horribly unflattering gym clothes while you did them. At Southglen South the gym clothes were made of this really icky yellow-and-green polyester that didn't even look good on the good-looking girls. It was especially ugly to see a whole roomful of girls dressed that way.

Beneath a cheery banner that read PRESIDENTIAL FITNESS TESTING WEEK, Josie sprinted up and down the basketball court with the rest of the girls. *How are they doing this?* she wondered, gasping for breath.

"Move it, Geller!" the gym teacher, Ms. Brown, shouted. "Move it! Move it!"

Josie plodded to a stop and grabbed the gym teacher by the shoulders. "Must—have—water . . . "

The gym teacher, hardened by years of inflicting such child abuse on generations of students, was unmoved. "What do I look like, your waitress? Now, you're gonna complete these sprints, 'cause if you don't, you fail. And if you fail gym, you're *never getting into college*!"

Josie stared in disbelief into the woman's cold, hard eyes. "Oh—my—God. You guys are still telling that lie?"

"That's it, Geller!" the gym teacher barked. "Drop and give me twenty!"

Josie dropped—more like fell—to the polished

gym floor and gave her twenty, one agonizing push-up at a time.

The smell of dust and wax and sweat was one you never forgot.

Finally, like even the worst nightmares, the school day came to an end. Physically and emotionally exhausted, Josie gathered her things from her locker and headed down the long, crowded hallway to freedom, clutching her reporter's notebook to her chest like a shield. Kids pushed and shoved around her. She valiantly tried to smile at a few, but no one smiled back. When she reached the main entrance, she sighed and stuffed the notebook into her bag.

Her first long, hard, brutal day of undercover investigative reporting had finally come to an end.

Her notebook was entirely blank.

Not a lot of material for a major, breaking, hard-hitting news story about high school.

Out in the parking lot Josie made a quick call to the office on her cell phone. Gus wasn't in, so she gave her idea for a story to his secretary. "And, Rhoda," she told her, "make sure Gus gets the whole message, okay? Yeah, bye."

Then she froze, phone still glued to her ear, as she stared at the area where she had parked her brother's car, Bambi, only hours before.

The space was empty.

Josie stuffed her phone back into her bag and looked around. The car couldn't be gone—that was impossible. She was just turned around, that was all. It was a pretty huge parking lot, she told herself; she'd just forgotten where she parked the car. She retraced her steps. She searched the parking lot space by space. But she found herself returning to the same spot.

Oh, God. Please. No. Not today.

But there was no doubt about it: Someone had stolen her brother's car.

7

"They do it to all the new kids."

Josie turned at the sound and found the girl from English class, the one in the orange Denominator sweatshirt, standing beside her, a look of sympathy on her face. Beyond her, several yards away, Josie saw a group of Denominator people gathered in one corner of the lot. Josie frowned and peered closer.

Unbelievable! They were unlocking a thick metal chain that had been wrapped around several cars tightly packed into a few spaces.

And this was supposed to be a good neighborhood!

"Who's 'they'?" Josie asked.

The girl shrugged toward the school building. Josie followed her gaze . . .

And gasped. The good-looking Guy from Ms.

Knox's class and several other students—Kristen, Kirsten, and Gibby among them—watched from a second-story window.

"Guy Perkins and his amazing Lemmings," the girl said with pure unadulterated hatred. "They push your car out of its space, hide it, then watch while you look for it."

Josie shielded her eyes and looked up at Guy and his friends—obviously enjoying her frustration and humiliation.

How could they? And, on a more practical note, *when* could they? Southglen South was guarded like a federal prison. How had Guy and his gang of glorified thugs managed to escape long enough during the day to move a car?

It was just as she'd known when she was in high school the first time: The popular kids lived by different rules.

The girl in the orange sweatshirt nodded toward her identically dressed friends. "We've taken to chaining our cars together for safety." She smiled. "I'm Aldys."

"I'm Josie." She tried to think of something nice to say to this friendly person. "Aldys is an interesting name."

"When it's not yours," Aldys replied wryly. She shrugged. "My mom was going through her Harlequin Romance phase."

"Try being named after a guitar-playing pussycat!" Josie commiserated.

Aldys frowned—she didn't get it.

Ooops! *Of course she doesn't get it,* Josie scolded herself. *Josie and the Pussycats* was a cartoon show on TV when *she* was a little kid. That was way before Aldys's time. Josie reminded herself that she'd have to watch popular-culture references that would date her and blow her cover. "Never mind," Josie said quickly. "That is so awful that they hide your cars."

"I guess," Aldys said. "Although what is truly awful is that with the combined intellectual effort of every kid in that room right now, they still would not know the difference between a synecdoche and hyperbole."

Josie laughed. "I know. It's pathetic."

Aldys nailed Josie with a tough stare.

"What?"

"Well, do *you*?"

Josie rolled her eyes. "Synecdoche uses a part to represent a whole—as in 'head of cattle,' whereas hyperbole is simple exaggeration, like 'I could eat a horse.'"

Aldys broke out into an approving grin. "Nice."

Josie knew she'd scored.

The girls looked back up at the window.

"How long will they watch us for?" Josie wondered.

"Until Guy tells them to go," Aldys said. "Once they watched me for like two hours. I found my car the next day in the T.J. Maxx parking lot."

"Why do they listen to Guy?" Josie asked.

Aldys gave her a major "Duh" look. "Because he's Guy Perkins."

Josie nodded. It was the same way in her old high school. Only then she'd never questioned it. But now, as a reporter, she had to. How did it happen? Who gave these people permission to push other kids around?

Maybe it was all the kids who got pushed around, she admitted. And the kids who'd go along with the Guys in the world just so they wouldn't be one of the kids who got pushed around.

Aldys paused then, studying Josie.

Josie went on alert; what had she said? Had she sounded too smart? Was Aldys beginning to suspect her?

But then Aldys smiled. "Listen, you want to walk to Na-Na's and get something to eat?"

It was a simple invitation, the kind friends exchanged easily. But to Josie, alone and feeling geeky in an alien world, it was a lifeline. "Yeah. Let's do that."

They walked the few blocks to Na-Na's, where they ordered a big plate of chili fries to share.

"Yeah, isn't it amazing that those guys are our

same age?" Aldys said between fries. "I mean, they just seem much younger, you know?"

"Oh—*I* know," Josie agreed.

Aldys shook her head. "It's really ironic."

Josie bit her lip. The misuse of *ironic* was one of her Top Ten pet peeves, especially since Alanis Morissette had to get into the act and get everyone confused. *Just let it go,* she told herself. *You've got a friend thing going here; don't blow it over a fine point of language.*

But she couldn't help herself. "Actually," she said, trying to keep her tone polite, "it's more paradoxical than ironic, since the first definition of *irony* is that you're conveying the opposite of the meaning you intend, and I think in this case your meaning and your intention are the same."

Aldys stopped with a chili fry halfway to her mouth as she pondered this and examined Josie's face.

Josie's heart skipped a beat. *You had to open your big mouth, didn't you?* she scolded herself.

But then Aldys smiled and nodded. "Nice."

"Thanks." Josie couldn't believe it—Aldys got it. Most of her coworkers at the paper didn't even get it. Josie sank back into the warm feeling of a new friendship.

A waiter placed two huge chocolate shakes in front of them on the table.

A new friend—and chocolate. It was turning into a pretty good afternoon.

"I'm going to be so happy to get to college," Aldys confided, as she played with her straw. "That's why I love coming in here—it's all college kids. You know, people who don't make fun of you for knowing the element table." She took a long draw on her shake. "I'm going to Northwestern."

"Hey!" Josie exclaimed. "I went to Northwestern!"

The confusion in Aldys's eyes instantly reminded Josie that she'd screwed up again. "Once," she added quickly. "To use the bathroom." Nervously she sucked hard on her milk shake and glanced out the window—and nearly choked. In one of those bizarre twists of coincidence, her brother Rob had just at that moment stopped at a red light . . . driving Josie's Buick, of course. But even more startling than that was what he had done to her nice, shiny, conservative car, the one she'd worked so hard to save up for: He'd painted on the side in huge white script the words:

THE TIKI POST

"Oh. My. God." *I'm gonna kill him. No—I'm not gonna kill him, I'm gonna let him suffer a while first . . . and then I'm gonna kill him. . . .* When she felt her paper milk-shake cup crumple beneath her clenched hands, she stopped and remembered Aldys. Josie let go of her cup, cleared her throat, and pasted a perky smile on her face. "You'll *really* like Northwestern."

They slurped on their shakes for a moment; then Josie, remembering the newspaper assignment that had led her here, asked, "So what are your hopes, your dreams? What do you want to be?"

Without hesitation Aldys responded, "Professor of medieval literature. Novelist. Weekend flautist."

A muffled ringing interrupted Josie's next question.

"I think your backpack is ringing," Aldys pointed out.

"Oh! Yeah." Josie dug in her bag for her cell phone. "Hello?"

"Geller! I got your message. What the hell kind of story are you pitching!?"

It was Gus.

Josie smiled awkwardly at Aldys and covered the mouthpiece with her hand. Gus was hollering so loudly, she wondered how much Aldys had heard. "It's . . . my dad," she fibbed. "He worries." Into the phone she said, "Hi, Dad. I miss you, too."

There was silence on the other end of the phone for a moment. Then Gus answered, "You are a sick puppy."

Josie excused herself and hurried to the back of

the restaurant, near the bank of pay phones, where she'd have some privacy to discuss her story idea.

"It's an exposé on cafeteria food," she explained.

"And you're leading with the terrible truth about coleslaw?" Gus exclaimed.

"Well, the bulk of it will be about the pimiento loaf—"

"Geller!" Gus shouted. "You wanna be a reporter? Take a look at what sells! Sex scandals. Bribery. People jumping off buildings. So unless a kid just killed himself because he was being paid to have sex with the school mascot in a big vat of this coleslaw, *you got nothing*!"

Gus hung up before Josie could respond. "You didn't taste the pimiento loaf," she said into the dead phone.

Back at the high school Josie and Aldys found Rob's yellow Bambi sitting in the middle of the track, with the school's marching band practicing their formations around it.

Blushing, apologizing, Josie got in the car to move it, only to find that it wouldn't start.

Aldys popped the hood. "They love to disconnect the battery, too." A few seconds later she slammed the hood and brushed off her hands. "Just so you know, I think they recalled these cars in 1974."

"Thanks."

"Sure. No problem."

With a wave, Aldys started to head back to the school parking lot to get her own car. But then she turned around. "Hey, Josie."

"Yeah?"

"How are you at calculus?"

Josie had always made straight A's in math, even calculus. She shrugged. "Pretty good."

"How would you like to join the Denominators? The Math Team could really use a new brain. We lost our best logarithm guy last year."

"College?" Josie guessed.

Aldys shook her head. "NASA. Plus we have these really fun pizza study groups, and we go to these all-county meets. And, I mean, not that you need it, and without sounding too much like the Godfather, I think we could offer you a certain amount of . . . 'protection,' if you know what I mean. We all kind of stick together and watch out for each other."

Josie smiled. "Yeah. I think I'd like that."

With a wave, Aldys jogged off toward her car.

Josie turned the key in the ignition, and Bambi rumbled to life—with no backfiring. Josie took it as a good sign.

As she drove home, she couldn't believe she'd been back in school only a single day. It seemed more like a week.

But she had a new friend, a new group to hang out with—and, with her new blond hair, she might look pretty good in an orange sweatshirt. At least she wouldn't have any fashion calls to get wrong.

She was feeling better already. Maybe tomorrow wouldn't be so bad.

Maybe this time around, she'd make it through high school okay.

8

It was a totally new experience.

Josie had never been in a club, clique, ensemble, or gang. She'd never made it onto any team.

But now her brains had found her a niche.

The Denominators wanted her.

She belonged.

She'd never felt as if she belonged back when she first went to high school. She'd never fit in anywhere, not in any group—not even with the pocket-protector patrol. She'd always felt as if she hovered on the outside, like in that children's game—a tisket, a tasket—she'd always felt outside the circle, with no clue as to how to break her way to the inside.

Even back at the paper she never truly fit in. Most of the reporters were interested in sensation and drama. They looked at her as some kind of old-maid schoolteacher control freak. Just because she loved the language. Just because she wanted to make things right.

But on her second day of high school at Southglen South, everything changed when the Denominators honored her with her very own Denominator sweatshirt.

When she pulled that orange sweatshirt on over her head, she felt infused with a strange power—a power that said I'm somebody. I belong here.

I have friends.

It didn't make her popular, of course. The popular kids wouldn't have anything to do with the Denominators. And it didn't make her immune to mistreatment. But it did help her endure the slings and arrows of teenage life.

Over the next few weeks Josie stayed so busy with homework—yes, she had to do the homework—and Denominator activities that she hardly even made it in to the newspaper office for staff meetings.

When the Denominators had a bake sale to raise money for trips, Josie came up with the sign:

π = 3.14159265

Pie = $.75

So what if nobody bought anything. They had a great time and got to eat a lot of brownies.

In the Math-a-lon Josie won her match against

the toughest member of the Digit team. So what if the only person who showed up at the gym to watch the event—outside of math teachers and a few parents—was the janitor sweeping up?

Being a member of the Denominators had become Josie's way of life; her job at the *Sun-Times* seemed very far away as she immersed herself in high school.

There was one other bright spot in her life, a special time each day that she looked forward to, no matter what else occurred. A place where she felt connected.

English class with Sam Coulson.

For most of an hour he led the class on a journey to loftier thoughts. So maybe most of the kids didn't go along for the ride, but it wasn't for Sam's lack of trying. And she, for one, was a willing traveler.

One day not long after she joined the Denominators, Aldys stood up in Sam's class, reading from her English textbook. "'All the world's a stage, and all the men and women merely players.'"

"Anyone have any idea what Shakespeare meant by that?" Sam asked.

No one moved. Except for a few kids near the back, who moved just enough to try to hide behind the student in front of them so they wouldn't get called on.

"Anyone?" Sam pressed. "Sera? . . . Megan? . . . Exchange student from an emerging Eastern Bloc country?"

A boy in the middle of the room smiled wildly and waved at the teacher, but couldn't speak enough English yet to answer.

Sam waved back at the exchange student, then looked around hopefully.

Josie hated having to keep a low profile in a favorite class. She slipped her hands under her knees to keep from raising one.

Sam answered his own question. "It's about disguise, playing a part. It's the theme of *As You Like It*. Can anyone tell me where we see that?"

Aldys raised her hand. "Well, Rosalind disguises herself as a man and escapes into the forest."

"Right," Sam said. "And it's when she's in costume that she can finally express her love for Orlando." He got up from his perch on his desk and began to walk around, looking into his students' eyes, trying to connect with them. "See, Shakespeare's making the point here that when we're disguised, we feel freer. We can do things we wouldn't do in ordinary life."

Josie squirmed uncomfortably in her seat. Being a spy for a major newspaper, she wasn't enjoying a discussion of disguises.

Sam strolled over to a huge guy, who Josie knew

played for the Southglen South football team. "Brett, when you go out on the football field in your uniform, what happens?"

Brett frowned, worried that it was a trick question. "We win?"

"You hit people," Sam said. "You yell. You touch other guys' butts."

The class laughed, but poor Brett looked horrified.

"But it's okay," Sam reassured him, "because you're in uniform. Disguise changes the rules." The teacher smiled and returned to his desk, excited now that the class seemed to be listening, really listening for a change. He propped himself against the edge of the desk and leaned forward, as if he were about to reveal a major secret. "The first season I played peewee hockey," he began—then he looked over his shoulder, as if not to let certain others hear—"frankly, I sucked. I was timid. Couldn't skate worth a damn."

The class laughed with him, finding the image of a bumbling young Sam Coulson humorous and endearing.

"So," Sam went on, "my dad went out and got me a new helmet signed by Gordie Howe!"

When no one recognized the famous player, Sam added, "He was the Tiger Woods of hockey."

That they got.

"Suddenly, when I put that helmet on . . . I was invincible. I skated hard. I checked other kids. I even got thrown out of a game for fighting. I played in that helmet for three years, until it cracked." Sam smiled, losing himself for a moment in the special memory.

Josie was delighted with the story, and forgetting to keep quiet, found herself asking softly, "Where's that helmet now?"

Sam's boyish smile faded, and he stood up from leaning against the desk, running a hand through his dark hair. "I don't know, actually," he said regretfully. "My girlfriend"—he swallowed—"threw it away."

The class gasped—even the normally bored ones—a tribute to Sam Coulson's ability to touch people's hearts with a simple story about a small boy.

How terrible, Josie thought and wanted to . . .

Nope. She sat up straight in her chair. No, she didn't. She didn't want to do anything. That was just a slip.

Sam was obviously uncomfortable with the personal turn the conversation had taken. "It wasn't her fault, really," he explained, forcing a laugh. "She just . . . likes to clean."

The students murmured to one another, still upset.

"The point here," Sam said, trying to get his students' minds back on Shakespeare, "is that disguise can be liberating, can get you to do things you never thought possible. For Rosalind, her male costume opened the possibility for the great love of her life."

Josie leaned forward in her desk, her chin propped in her hand, and refused to admit to herself that she was smitten with her English teacher. It was something only a silly teenager would do, not a twenty-five-year-old adult like she was. *It's the Shakespeare,* she told herself. *Shakespeare always makes you moony.*

"Josie, why don't you read from Act 5, Scene 2, Rosalind's speech?" Sam smiled at her with those big soulful eyes of his, and she found her legs turning to rubber. *Am I blushing?* she worried. But Sam nodded encouragingly at her, and she somehow got to her feet.

Josie found the place he'd requested and bit her lip. He would ask her to read one of her favorite passages—one of the most romantic Shakespeare had ever penned. She took a deep breath and shyly began to read: "'No sooner had they met but they looked; no sooner looked but they loved; no sooner loved but they sighed . . . '"

Like a drunk driver coming at you broadside, a memory of reading in front of another English class sent Josie reeling into the past. . . .

• • •

Josie is standing in front of a whole room of cold, heartless, staring eyes; her English teacher has unexpectedly called on her to read her homework assignment, a poem. A poem Josie should never have put onto paper, much less stand and read aloud. Her palms sweat and her hand trembles, rattling the paper. Somehow she forces herself to read in a soft voice:

"Does he notice me?
Does he hear my heart screaming his name?
Sometimes it's so loud I think
The gods can hear my pain.
His voice is so mellifluous,
Oh, to get just one small kiss."

The laughter begins by the end of line two, but she forces herself to ignore it. The teacher shushes them, but by the end of the poem the entire class is laughing and mocking her poetry.

Above her staining cheeks Josie's eyes slowly rise from the paper and peer through her glasses at the one person whose opinion really matters—the subject of the poem and the object of her affection: Billy Prince.

Her heart soars when she realizes he's not laughing, but smiling crookedly at her, with a thoughtful look in his eyes. Could it be true? Have her words somehow touched his heart?

Two days later Josie is in the library, bending over the color-coded index card system she's developed for her research paper. She glances up at the sound of her name.

Her friend Sheila comes running toward her as if her chubby form were being chased by demons, but a delighted grin spreads over her acne-ridden face. When she reaches Josie, she plops down in a chair and shoves the index cards aside.

"Hey—"

"Okay, what have you wanted for like forever, but you didn't think it would ever happen?" Sheila demands.

Josie studies her friend's face for a moment. What game is this? There are so many things. "That they'd start an Olympic team for grammar," she begins. "Like diagramming sentences and verb declensions and stuff. And I'm scouted for the team—just as an alternate, of course, because I'm so young. But then there's talk of me in the '96 games—"

"No, better. Something better!" Sheila looks as if she might explode.

Josie smiles dreamily. What's even better than that? Easy. "I'm the most popular girl in school, and Billy Prince is taking me to the prom." But then she shakes her head and laughs. Now, that's a really ridiculous dream.

Sheila nearly squeals. "Yes!"

"What?"

"Billy Prince is asking you to the prom!" Sheila blurts out.

Josie is stunned. How does her friend know? "Why?" she asks.

Sheila shrugs. "I don't know."

Josie searches her mind, thinking back over the past few days. Has there been a clue? A hint? What could have made him . . .

The poem!

"The poem!" Josie whispers in disbelief. "I knew he liked the poem!" And it begins to sink in! "Billy Prince is asking me to the prom."

"That's what I'm saying."

The two girls look at each other a moment, then jump up and down and hug each other.

What power there is in language well written! *Josie tells herself.* And for maybe the first time in her life, *she thinks,* I am a writer. . . .

The bell rang . . . and Josie looked around the classroom.

She was no longer seventeen, and Billy Prince was not in this English class. He was not about to ask her to the prom.

She glanced up at Sam. Had she made a fool of herself?

But Sam was smiling at her, in admiration of how she had read the passage.

Josie sighed and reached for her backpack as the rest of the students hurried to leave the class.

"Just a reminder," Sam called out over the noise of departing students. "Your paper is due in one week."

Josie left quickly, without looking at her English teacher. Aldys followed her as she raced to her locker.

Too late. Barbie and Ken had made it to her locker first and were well into their midmorning make-out session.

Josie watched them, frustrated, as the chipper voice of Sydney, student body president, came over the loudspeaker. "Hey, guys! Bad news—chem wing is closed. The Hazardous Materials Crew is on the way. Now, about the prom . . . "

As usual, the world stopped its gyrations. Even the make-out couple stopped theirs to listen.

"Please join a committee," Sydney said, "because we are going to kick Eastglen's butt and make Millennium the best prom ever!"

The hallway exploded in cheers.

"Rufus!" Guy exclaimed, shaking his head. "Prom is going to be rufus!"

Kristen frowned in confusion. "Rufus?"

"Yeah. I made it up. Start using it."

Josie darted in sideways to try to get her locker, but Barbie and Ken were faster.

She was just going to have to start carrying her books around with her every day.

"What is it with this school and prom?" Josie asked Aldys, as they walked to their next class. The prom had been big at her high school—it was probably big at most high schools. But here, it was like New Year's Eve, the World Series, and the Super Bowl rolled into one.

"Southglen South competes every year for best prom," Aldys explained. "We Denominators don't even go to the prom. But to everyone else it's huge."

Josie thought of her own prom, how excited she'd been, how much time she'd spent in searching for just the right dress, the pure magic of the night . . .

"Aldys," Josie said, trying to keep the bittersweet memories at bay, "don't miss your prom; it only happens once."

"This one is so hyped," Aldys complained. "We're tied for most wins with Eastglen East. This year's winner will determine the winner of the century. The theme is everything. So whatever Southglen picks has to be totally unique."

Across town, on the east side, an identical high-school hallway teeming with teenage angst and joy ground to a halt when their student body president spoke the magic word: *prom*.

"And this year's prom theme is—the millennium!"

The kids at Eastglen East High School erupted

in celebration. They knew their prom would be special, different, like no other prom in the world.

Halfway to class Josie realized that, in her daze, she'd forgotten something important. "I left my note cards in English," she told Aldys. "I'll see you later." She dashed down the hallway toward English class, hoping no one had decided to play good citizen—for once—and pick up her note cards to turn in. She didn't want anyone to read them. Her notes weren't about Shakespeare.

As she reached the class, she discovered that Sam was still there, sitting at his desk, engrossed in a book. At least, he was until she slid into the doorway.

"Whoa. *Déjà vu,*" he joked, since he'd just seen her.

Josie quickly glanced at her desk. Thank God. Her note cards were still there, lying facedown, untouched. She hoped.

"Sorry." Josie shrugged as she inched into the room. "Forgetful."

Then she noticed the book he was reading, and her face lit up. "Dorothy Parker—"

"You like her?"

"I love the way she writes."

Sam nodded his agreement with her mixed feelings. "Not the happiest of souls." He opened his book to the passage he'd been reading. "'Art is a form of catharsis, and love is a permanent flop.'" He chuckled at the melancholy line.

"But I think she wanted to be happy," Josie said, drawing toward him. "She was *writing* about love. Maybe deep down she was a real romantic."

Sam looked at her, puzzled.

"She did get married," Josie pointed out.

"Yeah, *twice*," Sam clarified with a grin. "Her writing is all about the realities of romance, that love is difficult. You have to make sacrifices."

"Well, I'd rather try and flop than settle," Josie said. "Love is too important to compromise."

They looked at each other then, and Josie suddenly realized she'd said too much, way too much for a conversation with a teacher. Her hands scooped up the forgotten note cards, and she backed toward the door. "Bye."

His finger holding his place in his forgotten book, Sam looked after her for a long time, mystified.

9

High school was never like this, Josie thought with a smile as she rode through the darkness on Saturday night.

Aldys was driving, Josie rode shotgun, and Tyke, Aldys's nine-year-old sister, rode in back, her head perched between the two big girls up front. They all had double-scoop ice cream cones and were singing "Free to Be You and Me" at the top of their lungs.

"See, aren't you guys glad you took a break from that Denominator stuff?" Tyke demanded. "I mean, you shouldn't be spending your Saturday night studying the *whole* time."

"We should be spending it thinking how we can better serve your baby-sitting needs?" Aldys asked.

Tyke grinned. "Yes. Exactly."

As they pulled up to a red light, Josie stared out into the cool night and spotted an old abandoned structure. Some kind of wall around what seemed to be a large empty field. Maybe an old ball field or something? Strange, she saw lights there . . . and people. What was going on?

She rolled down her window and peered through the darkness. She could see the shapes of people moving in the darkness, and in the field a big group of kids gathering around the light of a bonfire to talk. Some of them were drinking from beer cans. A few were making out.

"What's that?" Josie asked Aldys.

"That's the old drive-in," Aldys said. "They call it the Court. Now it's just a continuous party for Guy's group." It didn't take an investigative reporter to figure out how Aldys felt about the place.

As Josie scanned the faces in the crowd, she spotted some faces she knew—Gibby and Kristen talking by a car.

"Sometimes I wonder what they talk about," Aldys said.

"Yeah, I know," Josie agreed.

"I mean, what if they just *act* stupid to hide the fact that they're actually brainiacs with super powers, and they're plotting to take over the world and make my life hell until I die?"

Josie leaned closer to see if she could hear anything, some small scrap of their conversation, to hear what plots or philosophy they might be discussing. There, Gibby's voice, explaining something . . .

"No, no, no," she argued.

A debate perhaps?

"It's lather, rinse, repeat," Gibby insisted.

Ah, yes, one of the great issues of the millennium—how to achieve shiny hair.

Josie wondered what Aldys would say if she suggested they stop and go look around. Would Josie dare to do it? But she figured it wouldn't be such a hot place to take Tyke.

Suddenly a head shot in through Josie's window, and they all jumped.

Josie recognized the face. It looked menacing in the glow from the lights on the dashboard. Guy Perkins, invading their space. She could smell his cologne—good stuff—mixed with the odor of beer on his breath.

"Wow, if it isn't Alpo," Guy taunted Aldys. "Coming out to sniff some hydrants?"

Josie totally froze, but Aldys shot right back. "Oh, Guy, you on a little break from having an original thought? Oops, I forgot, that's all the time."

In the backseat Tyke snorted with laughter over

her big sister's cool insult. She got it; Josie got it. But Guy looked clueless—as if he couldn't quite figure out what Aldys had said. So he covered up with another insult. "You guys aren't seriously trying to hang out at the Court?"

"Oooh, cheap wine coolers and a fire in a trash can," Aldys said sarcastically. "Where do I sign up?"

Guy wasn't expecting such turn-on-a-dime wit. So he fought back with a vague: "And stay away from the prom!"

Aldys huffed. "Last time I checked—this was still a free country."

"'There's a land that I see,'" Tyke sang, "'where the children are free—'"

Guy leaned way in over Josie, glaring into Aldys's face. That seemed to spook Aldys, and she started to drive away, but Guy kept his head in the window and ran alongside the car.

"Look, geek, why don't you just go home and play with your calculator?" he shouted over the roar of the car engine. "Figure out how many lifetimes it will take you to get cool!"

Aldys looked scared and stepped on the gas.

As the car sped up, Guy pulled out.

Josie turned around and looked over the seat, out the back window. She could see Guy still standing there, legs spread wide, glaring at them, blazing like a devil in the glow from the car's red taillights.

A lump rose in her throat. *Why does he hate us so much?* she wondered. *Why do any of them—the cool kids, the kids who seem to have everything—why do they hate us losers so damn much?*

It was a mystery she felt she would never unravel, even if she went to high school a thousand times.

Her eyes fell on Tyke then. The poor kid had grown as quiet as a mouse, hugging her knees to her chest, the words of her happy song—"free to be you and me"—all forgotten, her eyes two big saucers as she tried to make sense out of what she'd seen and heard. Her forgotten ice-cream cone dripped on the floorboard.

Josie smiled at her, trying to tell her that everything was all right, and reached back to ruffle the top of her head. Tyke rewarded her with a small smile.

Josie turned around in her seat. Her own ice cream was melting, and she felt around on the floor for the handful of napkins she'd picked up at the store. But when she glanced at Aldys, she forgot all about her ice cream. Her friend's eyes were focused straight ahead on the road, her knuckles white as she gripped the steering wheel, her ice cream dropped upside down and melting on the section of the front seat that separated them. She acted calm, but in the light from the dashboard Josie could see the pain in those eyes. A pain Josie easily recognized. A pain she knew by heart.

"Have you ever wanted to go to the Court?" she asked softly.

"Are you kidding?" Aldys lied, and laughed—a little too loudly. "It's lame. All they do is stand around and get drunk. It's so lame."

"It is?"

"Yes, it's lame," Aldys repeated.

"Yeah, it sounds lame," Josie agreed. "Why would we want to go there and stand around?"

"Exactly."

Josie gathered up their melted ice-cream cones and tossed them as the three girls drove home in silence through the dark streets.

10

Sunday morning. Josie felt strange being in the office, especially on a Sunday morning. Sunday mornings were usually pretty quiet around a morning newspaper.

But not this morning. Gus's shouts of outrage could wake the gargoyles on the building across the street.

She knew she was about to get yelled at; she just wasn't sure why yet. For some reason, as she entered her boss's office and sat down in front of his desk, she thought of Sam Coulson's paper cups of coffee and wished she'd thought to pick up a cup on her way in.

Gus didn't beat around the bush—he never did. He picked up a hefty Sunday newspaper and slammed it onto his desk for her to see. The headline read:

THE COURT—SITE FOR PARTIES, DRUGS, AND WEEKEND ARRESTS

Totally surprised, Josie picked up the newspaper and began reading intently.

"Josie, I am appalled," Gus said.

"Jeez, so am I," she agreed, still reading. "I had no idea that these kids—let's see, turn to page A14 —" She opened the paper up in front of her, searching for the jump head, but jumped when Gus snatched the entire newspaper from her hands.

She didn't like the looks of Gus's face. It was red, really red, only about three shades shy of total rage. She had a feeling this was not going to be a good meeting.

"Nooooo," he said with exaggerated patience, trying to hang on to his temper, "I am appalled that I have a reporter in *there, undercover*, for almost *three weeks* now—and I had to read about this in the *Tribune*!"

"Oh. Right."

Gus tried to fold up the newspaper, but he was so mad, he succeeded only in mangling it. Josie tried to help him, but that only made him angrier, and he grabbed it away and started reading again, with half the pages slipping to the floor.

"Responding officers found minors, marijuana, and cheap wine coolers . . . "

Aha, Aldys was right, Josie thought.

". . . when they responded to a call to break up a party at what Southglen High schoolers have come to call the Court. Seventeen-year-old Kristen Davis says, 'Yeah, everyone who's anyone is at the Court on Saturday night.'"

Josie couldn't believe it. "Kristen got a quote?" she exclaimed.

Gus's glare was lethal.

"Yes, um, she's right." Josie shifted to her mature professional journalist voice. "I have learned it is a very popular place for the young people to go."

"Have you been there?" he demanded.

"Uh, no," Josie admitted. She didn't think driving by and getting chased away by Guy would count.

"Have you been to any parties?"

"Well . . ." Josie shifted uncomfortably in her chair. "How would you define 'parties'? Because we ordered a deli platter at this one Denominator drill session—"

Her boss looked as if he were about to burst into flames. Hands trembling in barely suppressed rage, he jerked open the newspaper again, found the part he was searching for, and shoved it in Josie's face.

She backed up a bit so she could focus—and

winced. It was a picture of all the popular kids at Southglen—Kirsten, Kristen, Gibby, Guy . . . standing around the bonfire at the Court, posing for the *Tribune*'s photographer, brazenly toasting him with their beers.

Gus shook the paper in her face. "*This* is where the stories are," he growled, then gave her his new assignment. "You are going to become *friends* with these people. You are going to *party* with them. You are going to hang out with them on *weekends*. When they go to the prom, you are going to be in their *same—damn—LIMO*!"

Impossible. That's all there was to it. It was impossible for her to become friends with the popular kids. "Gus, I . . ." How could she explain? "The popular kids and I, we just don't—I mean . . . I don't think I can do this."

"Do you even know these kids?" he demanded, pointing at the picture in the paper.

Josie gave him the iffy sign with her hand. "They hid my car. . . ."

Gus didn't crack a smile. He splayed his hands out on his desk and leaned toward her and spoke very clearly and distinctly. "Get to know them. Very well. Your job and my job depends on it."

Josie cleared her throat and looked down at her nails. "*Depend* on it," she said in a very tiny voice.

Gus stared at her, confused.

"No *s*," she practically whispered. "Your subject is plural—"

"OUT!"

Josie snagged her backpack and was out of his office before his shout had finished reverberating off the walls.

She shot out of there so fast she didn't even stop to say hi to Anita. But that was okay. Anita was busy watching Roger from op-ed stroll toward her cubicle.

Anita and Roger smiled flirtatiously at each other for a full ten seconds before either of them spoke.

"Hi, Roger from op-ed," Anita said breathlessly.

"Hi, Anita from classifieds," Roger said huskily. "We still on for tonight?" he asked with a wink.

Anita winked back. "Of course . . . "

To seal the deal, Roger leaned over and kissed her, right in the middle of her cubicle.

How romantic, she thought. *How* . . .

Anita suddenly pulled back from the kiss, totally confused. For some reason Josie's silly romantic words echoed through her mind. She tried to ignore them, but they wouldn't go away. . . .

"You kiss someone, and it's like the world around you gets all hazy . . . and you know that one person is the person you're meant to be kissing the rest of your life. And for that one moment you've been given this amazing gift and

you want to laugh and cry at the same time because you're so lucky you found it, and so scared that it will all go away."

With a shake of her hair, she grabbed Roger's face in both hands and kissed him again, hard and with feeling.

She broke it off and dropped her hands, stunned.

Nothing.

None of that crazy wonderful stuff that Josie had talked about. And then she couldn't believe the words coming out of her mouth. "Y'know what?" she told Roger. "No, I don't think we are on. I think I have to stay home." As the words hung in the air between them, she began to like the sound of them more and more, enjoyed how they instantly wiped that smug, flirtatious look from his face.

"Yeah," she said with even more conviction, "I'm staying home! I don't know what I'll do there, but I'm gonna do it."

She crossed her arms and sat back in her chair, waiting to hear what he'd say to that.

He didn't say anything. He just turned on his heel and walked away. "Freak," he muttered under his breath.

Josie stood on her parents' doorstep, having a major life crisis. She bet there weren't too many people who'd ever had to suffer over peer pressure and career pressure at the same time. It was like living two lives at once—and both of them were going very badly just then.

Josie leaned on the doorbell till her brother Rob opened the door.

God, she thought when she saw that he was still wearing his Tiki Post clothes, *does he sleep in those things?* "Are Mom and Dad here?" she asked right off.

"No. They're at the Franklin Mint Expo at the Skokie Holiday Inn."

"Good." Her problems might have brought her to her parents' doorstep, but the last people she wanted to talk to right now were her mom and dad. Her brother wouldn't really be near the top of the list, either, but he would have to do. She shoved past her brother, through the foyer, and into the den, where a major-league baseball game was playing on the TV. She planted herself on the couch, reached for the remote, and clicked off the TV.

"I can't do it," she complained to her brother, getting right to the point. "I thought I could, but I can't. I give up—I'm never going to be a reporter." She made an exasperated choking kind of sound and buried her face in her hands.

Rob sat down and stared thoughtfully at the now-blank TV screen. "Um, did you happen to catch the score?"

Josie's scathing look made him regret even thinking the word *baseball* while his sister was in the room. "No, I mean, no big whoop." He forgot the TV and gave his sister his full attention.

"I can't do this." With a huge sigh she reached into her purse and pulled out the neatly folded newspaper article about the kids at Southglen getting in trouble at the Court.

Rob stared intently at the photo of the kids around the bonfire, shaking his head. "These girls are high schoolers? Damn, we've got some underage hotties on our hands here!"

Josie ignored his remark and went on with her problems. "Gus insists that I become friends with these kids. The popular kids." She felt like ripping the paper to shreds. "It's impossible."

"Why is that impossible?"

Tears welled in the corners of Josie's eyes. How could she make her brother understand what it was like for her? "Rob, you don't know how it was for me back in high school. No one ever threw juice boxes at you in the hallway. You never dreamed about being popular—you already were. All I wanted was to be accepted, and they just tortured me. I can't do all that again. I can't go back to Southglen South."

"Oh, my God." Rob put a comforting hand on his sister's shoulder. "You're at Southglen South?"

She nodded; maybe he could understand after all.

"Whoa. They have a killer baseball team!"

Josie scowled. "Rob. Please focus."

Rob smiled and put his arm around her. "Jos, you've been to college, you're successful, you wash your hair now—you're not Josie Grossie anymore."

"Don't you realize how much I wanted to be you in high school?" she told him. "Just for *one minute* to feel what it was like to be popular?"

"Come on!" Rob said encouragingly. "It's not that hard. All you need is one person."

She shot him a look of skepticism.

"Believe me. Once the right person thinks you're cool, you're in. Everyone else will be too scared to question it."

"Is that true?"

Rob nodded. "Little-known fact."

Josie chewed her thumbnail, absorbing this information. She still didn't think she could do it, no matter what he said. But if she didn't, she'd lose one of the best things that had ever happened to her. Her copyediting job at the *Sun-Times*.

"Look," her brother said gently, "don't you wanna show them—Gus, Billy Prince, *yourself*—that you're not freaked out by the cool kids anymore? That you can go in there, be friends with them, and get your story?"

"Yes, desperately."

"Plus," he added wistfully, "if you quit, you're no better than me."

"Better than *I*," she corrected.

Rob hit her with a couch pillow. "That's the spirit!"

11

The next morning Josie arrived at the school parking lot with new determination, new energy, and a new pair of too-high platform shoes that she hoped would help get her a foot in the door with the popular girls. Sure she felt uncomfortable in the midriff-baring top she'd chosen, but she'd convinced herself that her art was worth the sacrifice.

She nearly fell off her platforms, though, when she saw a guy she knew from the *Sun-Times* staff wave at her from the open door of a van. She looked around, hoping none of the students saw her, but then didn't know whether to feel glad or depressed that no one seemed to notice her at all.

"George!" she whispered when she reached the van. "What are you doing here?"

"Just get in the van, Josie."

Josie checked her watch; she didn't have much time before the first bell rang. She hoped this wouldn't take long. But she figured George wouldn't be here unless it was important.

Josie climbed into the van and marveled at George's decorating style: high-tech surveillance wonderland meets seventies living room. His wall of electronics equipment looked like a section at Radio Shack. He had shag carpeting, a minifridge. Slow, soulful music played on the CD player.

George wrapped a tiny wire around Josie's wrist, then pinned a kid's plastic "captain's wings" on her collar.

"What is this?" she asked, worried.

"Hidden camera," he explained.

"Wings?"

"We used it for our exposé on overweight flight attendants. Remember that story: 'Is That Why They Never Give You a Second Bag of Nuts?'"

Josie remembered, but she didn't like the idea of recording the kids at school. The *60 Minutes* style of surprising people with hidden cameras had always made her feel uncomfortable, as if there was something not quite honorable about it. She pulled her arm out of George's grasp and shook her head. "I'm not doing this until I speak with Gus."

"Geller, stop being a pain in the ass!"

Josie looked all around her. *Did Gus actually leave the newsroom? Is he hiding somewhere here now?* "Gus?" she whispered.

"No, it's the Great and Powerful Oz!" he snapped. He was speaking to her from his office through a speaker. "Now listen—you're in over your head. This is how it's gonna work. I review the tapes, I find your story."

Josie didn't like losing control of her story. And the whole thing felt so sneaky, so . . . dishonest.

But then going undercover and pretending to be a high-school student when you were a twenty-five-year-old copy editor was pretty sneaky and dishonest to begin with.

"What if I say no?"

"I bet *Good Housekeeping* would go gaga over the coleslaw piece. . . ."

Josie caught his drift and made a quick decision: to keep receiving a paycheck.

George double-checked her wires, complimented her on her platforms, then sent her out to begin her first broadcast of Josie Geller TV.

Now she knew there was something worse than going to high school. Something worse than going to high school for the second time. And that was having an audience watch you do it.

As she neared the school, Josie spotted Kirsten, Kristen, and Gibby walking up the crowded steps to the front of the school.

"Hey! Kirsten, Kristen, Gibby!" she called out. "What's up, girlfriends?"

The girls turned around and gave her an icy stare, but Josie didn't see it—because she was too busy tripping on a backpack someone had left on the steps.

Back in the van George winced when the wings minicamera pinned to Josie's midriff-baring shirt told him she'd bit the cement.

"I'm okay," he heard her whisper.

George had a feeling that compared to the fat-flight-attendant story, Josie's was going to be a lot more painful.

She was standing, reading her paper in Mr. Coulson's class.

"And so it is Rosalind, in disguise, who is best able to see through the disguise of others. To say to Phebe, 'Mistress, know yourself,' to look at love from every angle, and to realize, finally, that she is in love with Orlando—"

The bell rang, and the rest of the class got a head start on dashing from the classroom. Josie quickly grabbed her things and hurried to catch up with the Cool Girls. "Hey, guys, wait up—"

They didn't slow down; in fact, it seemed as if they even sped up.

"Hey, Josie, hold on."

Josie was disappointed to miss her chance to chase down the popular girls, but she figured Sam wanted to comment on the paper she'd just read. But when she turned and saw the probing look in his eyes, she panicked.

He closed the door firmly.

Uh-oh. Double panic.

"You've been hiding something from everyone," he said in a low voice.

Josie couldn't read his expression. What did he know? And what would he do with that information? Could she fake him out? Maybe she should just leave and keep on running till she came to the unemployment line.

She decided to play it cool. Partly because her feet seemed to be rooted to the floor. She cleared her throat. "Oh . . . I don't think so."

Brilliant answer, she scolded herself. She'd pulled a near-perfect score on the language section of the SAT eight years ago—and these were the best words she could pull out of her vocabulary list in time of emergency?

"Josie, c'mon," Sam said. His voice was deep and insistent; she felt his eyes could see through to her bones. "I know you lied to Knox."

Josie's heart stopped.

Sam waited for her to say something, but she didn't know what to say—couldn't speak—so when she simply stared back at him, helplessly, he said at last, "You aren't from Bali, are you?"

The panic attack started at the bottom of her spine, then spread up her back to her arms, making her hands tremble. What would happen to her if he revealed her deception? She'd never thought to ask Gus if they were breaking any kind of law here. Could she be arrested for lying about her age?

Didn't women do that all the time?

She closed her eyes. The words "Gus is going to kill me" escaped from her lips on a whisper.

"I checked your transcripts," Sam revealed; then added more gently, "Josie, look at me—"

She raised her terrified eyes to his strong, sure, beautiful ones.

"There's nothing wrong with being from Scranton, Pennsylvania," he said kindly.

Josie's mouth gaped open.

Okay, let's have an instant replay here: There's nothing wrong with being from Scranton, Pennsylvania?

That was the lie he'd uncovered? He didn't know she was really a twentysomething copyediting reporter wanna-be masquerading as a seventeen-year-old geek?

Sam clasped his hands together, earnest in his desire to help this young student. "You don't need to worry that your college applications won't be exotic enough to get into the Ivy League schools," he assured her. Then he frowned in puzzlement as her previous remark sank in. "Who's Gus?"

Gus? Did I mention Gus? "My, uh . . . *Uncle* Gus," Josie made up real quick. She was becoming quite handy at fibbing on her feet. "He . . . feels college is a real waste of time," she embellished. *Keep going with the fabrications, girl, and you'll have the beginning of a good short story!*

"What?" Sam exclaimed. He couldn't believe anyone would still feel that way, here at the beginning of the millennium, when technology, politics, and ideas were about to take a quantum leap. Especially when Josie showed such intellectual promise. "Please let me talk to him before you make your decision," he insisted. "*Promise* me you'll think about college. I'm not taking no for an answer."

Think about college? All she could think about was college, the four years she already spent at college, at Northwestern, and what he'd think if he knew she'd already graduated—cum laude, she might add.

So she just nodded. "Okay. Maybe."

"*Promise.*"

His stern tone startled her, and she gazed up

into his eyes. His big, beautiful, sensitive, caring eyes that made her wish she'd met him in her other life, not while she was masquerading as an untouchable teen. . . .

The thought startled her, and she blushed at the audacity of it.

"I promise," she whispered.

And for a moment their eyes locked, and the chalkboards and the grade books faded into oblivion, and the school bell calling them to their assigned roles went totally ignored.

Watching in his shag-carpeted seventies dream pad, George could only murmur one thing. "Uh-oh."

Work could wait, Anita thought. She sat on the edge of Gus Strauss's desk in his office in the *Sun-Times* building, captivated by the love scene taking place on her boss's TV screen. But this was no ordinary daytime drama—this was *way* better than the soaps.

This was the life and loves of her best friend Josie Geller being played out up close and in full color. And she had a feeling it was about to lose its TV-17 rating.

Anita slowly slipped another spoonful of mocha yogurt into her mouth and sighed. If she'd ever had a teacher as babelicious as Sam Coulson, she never would have graduated—by choice. She peered at the screen. She wondered how long those two could stand there like that without moving. . . . She checked the second hand on her watch and started timing them.

But then Gus stormed in and ruined all the fun. "Showtime's over!" he shouted, turning off the monitor. "Come on—move it! Back to work!"

Anita slid off his desk with a dreamy look on her face, slowly stirring her creamy cup of yogurt. "Gus, have you ever been in love?"

"Leave."

Anita huffed and straightened her slim skirt, her whole mood ruined. "Oh, give it up, Gus. I'm just making conversation."

Gus shook his head and moved some papers around on his desk. "Love. Who knows what that is? Now, circulation, deadlines—those I understand."

Anita put one hand on her hip and stepped back to give her grouchy, fashion-challenged but not altogether unattractive boss the once-over. "You should go out every now and then, Gus. With some new ties, the girls would be all over you."

Gus tried not to look at his tie, but he couldn't help himself. He peeked down at the long, slightly rumpled strip of material. *What's wrong with my ties?* he wondered, but he couldn't totally hide his smile at Anita's teasing remark—she was teasing him, wasn't she? "Go away," he said gruffly. "I have enough work here to last me all night."

Anita suddenly found herself leaning across his desk, with her hands splayed out on those unimportant papers. "Listen . . . I don't have any plans—you want some help?"

Gus eyed her in surprise. "No Roger from op-ed?"

"Nope." Anita smiled crookedly.

Well, well, well, Gus thought, straightening his tie. *This is late-breaking news. . . .*

12

Josie thought she'd throw up.

She approached the couple using her locker door for a make-out springboard—at least she thought it was a couple; it was hard to tell where one ended and the other began—and tapped what she thought might be the shoulder of the boy. "Excuse me. Hi. Do you guys have a schedule I could work around?"

The boy tore himself away long enough to give her a blank look, then turned back to his girlfriend.

She must have sucked his brains out with that last kiss, Josie stewed.

Yeah, she was great at snappy comebacks in her head. Too bad she was too chicken to say them out loud. These guys' hormones were beginning to put a dent in her grades.

Maybe it's time to check the office about a locker reassignment. . . .

"Hey, where's your sweatshirt?"

Josie jumped at the accusation and whirled around to find Aldys, wearing her ever-present orange sweatshirt decorated with her beloved math medals.

Not feeling guilty, are you, Jos? she asked herself dryly. This was definitely going to be the tricky part of her new hang-with-the-Cool-Kids assignment. Aldys had been a good friend to her when no one else would even look at her, except to laugh. But how could she still hang with Aldys and the Denominators when she needed to convince the popular kids that she was cool enough to hang with them?

Fact of life: She couldn't. The ancient rules of adolescent society decreed that she couldn't be a subset of two totally opposite groups. She had to pick just one—and Gus had chosen for her. Josie searched for the words that would make everything right, to explain why she'd laid the orange token of friendship and camaraderie aside. . . . But in her nervousness she blurted out the handiest lie: "I, uh . . . must have forgotten."

Aldys smiled. "No biggie."

See? Josie reassured herself. *Aldys is an intelligent, rational person. This is going to be all right.*

"I have an extra in my locker," Aldys offered. "I'll get it for you."

Ewww. Maybe it was going to be a little messy after all.

"Oh, I almost forgot," Aldys said. "I'll see you tonight at Na-Na's. Seven-thirty, right?"

Tonight? Seven-thirty?

Josie's confusion must have shown on her face, because Aldys rolled her eyes good-naturedly. "Remember that poet that we liked—the reading he's doing at Na-Na's? I got us tickets?"

Josie snapped her fingers. "Right. Right. Seven-thirty."

A hurt look fell across Aldys's face like a shadow.

Josie knew she sensed a change, but felt helpless to reassure her.

Aldys looked down. "I'm late for lab." And then she took off.

Josie felt like a rat, but what could she do? Better a rat than an unemployed mouse, right? Maybe.

You've got a job to do, she reminded herself sternly. *You're an adult—an adult who left these childish games behind years ago. You want to be a reporter so bad? Go find something to report on.*

With a shake of her head, she began to search

the hallway for signs of popular life. She found all her main targets—Guy, Kristen, Kirsten, Gibby, and their fan clubs—reading a flyer taped to the wall.

"That is gonna be such a sweet show," Guy said, shaking his head.

"Oh, yeah, man," said a kid named Tommy. "I'll drive."

"It's going to be Ruflicious," a guy named Jason remarked.

Guy frowned. "You're using it wrong!"

They moved off en masse, almost as if chained together like the Denominators' cars, discussing the appropriate ways to utilize Guy's newly coined slang.

Josie hurried over to read the flyer they'd been reading: OZOMATLI TONIGHT AS DELLOSER HALL.

Josie smiled. She knew one loser who was going to show up and graduate into the in crowd.

13

Bambi got Josie to Delloser about 8:45. Josie parked, checked her hair and makeup in Bambi's rearview mirror, and then forced herself to get out of the car.

She'd never been much of a club hopper. It took some guts to approach the door of the dark, funky-looking place alone.

But she could do it. If Woodward and Bernstein could endure dark, empty parking decks to talk to Deep Throat, if CNN journalists could broadcast the news while Gulf War SCUD missiles screamed through the skies behind them, if Dustin Hoffman could pass himself off as a woman . . . she could pretend to be a teenager and enter a hip club to get the news.

She approached the door and dug money from her jeans pocket to pay the cover charge.

"You drinking?" the bouncer demanded.

"I am *not* twenty-one," Josie insisted, trying to look insulted. "I am only seventeen, and I still attend high school."

The bouncer stared. That was a new one. Usually he had to screw around with kids claiming to be a heck of a lot older than they really were—this one was trying to *prove* she was too young to drink? Go figure.

He shrugged and stamped her hand with the name of the club: DELLOSER.

.

Two of Josie's classmates came in behind her: Stoned and More Stoned.

"Two of you?" the bouncer asked, as he held out his beefy hand for their money.

The two stoners swayed a moment, thinking—counting maybe. Then looked at each other in horror. "Oh, dude—!"

They stumbled back out into the dark parking lot.

Must have forgotten Jed at the 7-Eleven again, Josie guessed.

Josie entered the small, smoky club and looked around. Ozomatli was already deep into a set, and the crowd was already into a deep groove. Looking around for familiar faces from school, she approached the bar to get something with ice to drink.

A moment later she sensed someone looking at her, someone standing right next to her at the bar, too close to look casually, so she kept her eyes trained on the other end of the bar.

Then she felt his hand on her arm. Yikes.

But then he spoke. "Josie—out on a school night."

She looked up into the eyes that she'd lost herself in only hours ago at the end of English class. Sam Coulson. Sitting there all alone and looking even more wonderful out of the classroom.

Josie warmed to his smile and leaned toward him to say something over the loud music.

But then she saw an arm snake around his shoulders. A woman's arm. An arm that was attached to a very polished, attractive woman, who had materialized out of thin air.

"That bathroom is *disgusting*," she complained.

Josie's smiled vanished. *Is he with this "charming" person?*

"Hey," Sam said to Josie. "I'd like you to meet Lara."

"His *girlfriend*," Lara clarified, studying Josie's face.

Josie told her heart not to ache over the news. She knew he had a girlfriend, he'd told them all in class. Somehow, she hadn't pictured a woman who looked like this.

"She's visiting from New York," Sam explained. He turned to Lara. "Josie's a student of mine."

"Hi, it's nice to meet you!" The band had turned up the volume, and Josie spoke loudly to be heard.

Lara made a face. "What?"

"I said 'hi there!'"

"I'm sorry. I just can't think in here." She looked at her boyfriend as if he were an unruly little boy. "No offense, Sam, I know you love it, but I hope you get this out of your system by the time you move to New York." She smiled at Josie. "My firm has season tickets to the Met."

"Oh, I love baseball," Josie joked.

Sam laughed, but Lara didn't seem to get it. "Nice to meet you," she said in a voice that said it wasn't really. Sam waved to Josie as Lara dragged him off into the crowd.

Somehow, Josie had no trouble at all believing that Lara was the woman who had thrown out Sam's beloved Gordie Howe helmet.

Loud laughter captured her attention, and she turned her head.

Guy and his friends had gathered around a large round table—with one empty seat. Josie aimed for it and tried to forge a path through the crowd. But by the time she reached their table, they'd rearranged

◀ Drew Barrymore plays Josie Geller, a compulsively neat, twenty-five-year-old copy editor and reporter wanna-be for the *Chicago Sun-Times*.

▼ Josie gets her big break as a reporter. She's going undercover as a student at the local high school.

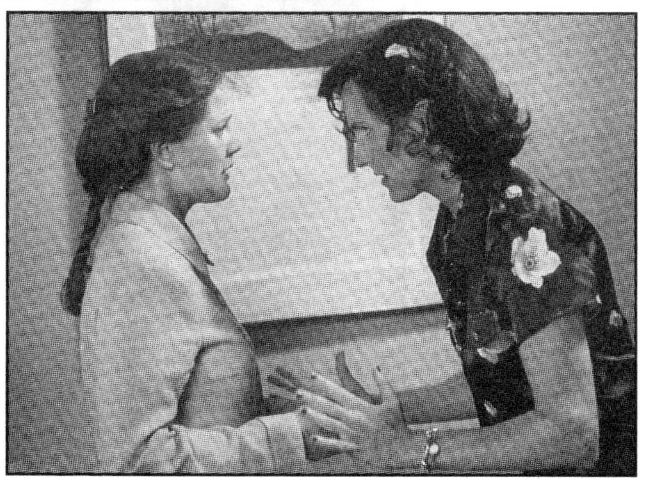

▲ High school—and the cool kids—are just as intimidating as Josie remembers.

▶ Despite her intensive shopping and new look, Josie can't quite fit in the way she wants.

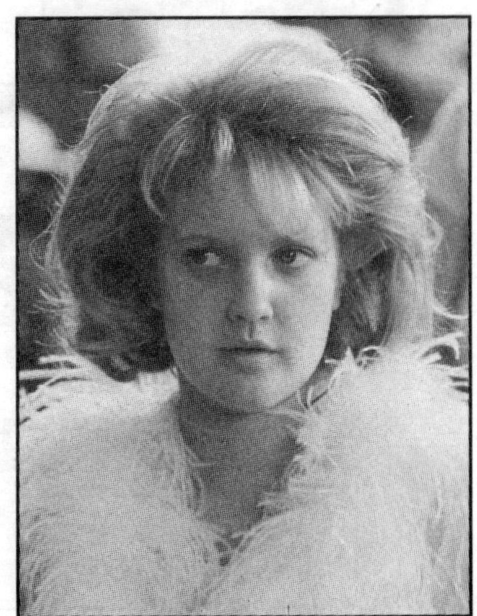

▲ But Josie quickly makes friends with the school geeks—the Denominators.

▶ Leelee Sobieski plays Aldys, Josie's best friend on her second time through high school.

▲ But best of all, Josie finds herself loving her classes with Sam …

▼ … that is, with Mr. Coulson, the handsome, idealistic English teacher played by Michael Vartan.

▲ Josie's boss ups the pressure on her to get a hot story. If she fails, they'll both be fired.

▼ Josie's brother Rob (David Arquette) comes to her rescue.

▼ With the aid of a few strategic lies by Rob, Josie is magically part of the cool group.

▲ Josie is crowned queen of the senior prom, her dream come true—or is it?

◀ There are things way more important than being popular, like real friendship … and love.

▼ Josie finds her story.

Josie discovers that "... inside everyone is a loser afraid to be loved, and out there is the one person who can kiss us and make it all better."

themselves somehow so that the seat had disappeared. It was as if their geek buster had picked up her signal.

Pulitzer Prize, pay raise, the respect and admiration of all my peers . . . These were the thoughts that kept Josie intent on her mission, and, undeterred, she simply pounced on a seat at the next table.

Proud of her determination, Josie glanced around to smile at her tablemates: half a dozen Rastafarians grooving in unison, surrounded by a cloud of sweet-smelling smoke.

Josie had copyedited an article on Rastafarians once. But she had never met a person of their persuasion in person. They had the kind of strong presence that made a shy girl like Josie feel awkward and out of place. But she tried. "Hi. Uh, is it okay if I sit here?"

"Oh, ya, mon," the Rastafarian to her left said. "We accept all peoples. We are all about da love."

Oh. How nice. The group seemed to bob up and down as one to the music, like a backup group in rehearsal, and she found herself drawn into the rhythmic motion, a gentle movement that instantly began to mellow her out.

She glanced over at Guy's table and was surprised to see them passing a small joint around.

Josie freaked and shot a glance at the burly bouncer. He didn't bat an eye. The waiters and waitresses seemed oblivious, too. Josie couldn't believe it. Was she the only person in here who found this activity a little . . . illegal?

She wondered what Sam's reaction would be, but couldn't see him anywhere in the crowd. Perhaps Lara had made him leave.

Josie turned back to the problem at hand. She was trying to prove how cool she was to Guy and his friends. And she was over twenty-one—the legal drinking age. Of course, what these kids were doing wasn't legal at any age.

Gus seemed to want her to get her story at any cost. Would he consider this research?

She bit her lip. What she should do? She ought to get up and leave immediately.

Then she heard the words Gus had thrown at her in his office not so many weeks ago. *"Geller, you don't want a reporter's life. They're very . . . messy. You're about order. Control. . . "*

"Hey—I can be out of control," she had told him.

She'd known then he didn't believe her.

Maybe tonight was the night to show him.

Outside in the *Sun-Times* news van George slipped his arm around his foxy date and relaxed back into the plump cushions of the comfortable couch, groovin' to the free concert coming over the monitor. Now this was a job! He almost felt guilty for getting paid to do this. But hey, who was he to question his employer's judgment?

He and his lady rubbed noses and shared a light kiss . . . .*Heaven,* George thought. He turned back to the screen, head still bobbing to the music—and nearly choked.

Oh, Lord. Tell me I'm dreaming! George sat up fast and leaned toward the monitor for a closer look. Through the smoky haze he saw a joint the size of Cuba make its way around the Rastafarians' table. And then he saw a pale, slender hand—a sweet innocent hand that should be holding nothing more sinister than a copy editor's pencil—reach out and take it.

George buried his face with his hands. *I can't look. . . .*

Josie felt insanely happy. She was *really* getting into this place. She felt as if she were riding the music on a little magic carpet of smoke. Josie laughed hysterically. She'd have to tell Rob. No! He'd have a fit. Yes! It'd be worth it to see him have a fit!

Let's see, where was I? The punch line! The punch line of the joke.

Giggling, she looked around at her dear, wonderful new friends, the Rastafarians. They'd stopped bobbing, and they were staring at her. They must be dying to hear the punch line.

She let them have it.

They still didn't move.

"Get it? *Get it!"* she shrieked. *"He was a firecracker!"* Josie practically fell off her chair laughing. But these guys just sat there as if they were at a funeral or something.

Maybe they didn't hear me. She lifted up the dreadlocks of the nearest one and shouted into his ear, "A *firecracker!"*

The guy winced and pulled away from her, then turned to the man sitting next to him. "I *don't* love her."

All his friends nodded in agreement.

Suddenly the first strains of "Cut Chemist Suite" blasted through the room.

"Oh, my God!" Josie shouted. "This music *rules!"*

She leaped onto the table and started dancing, knocking over drinks. Stepping on fingers. Stepping into something squishy—pie, maybe?—but even though she was starving, she was having too much fun to stop dancing.

See, Mr. Gus Strauss? she wanted to shout to the editor all the way across town to his square little office. *Little shy Josie Geller is Capital O, Capital O, Capital C—Out Of Control! Whatdya think about them apples, baby?*

Of course, if she were capitalizing "Out of Control" on paper, she wouldn't actually cap the second *O,* because *of* was a preposition. . . .

Oh, shut up, Geller! she told herself, and misspelled three words on purpose—*irresistable, fuschia,* and *manuveur*—just to prove to herself that she was truly out of control.

The next thing she knew she was onstage with the band—singing at the top of her lungs (even though she didn't know the words), playing the bongos (even though she'd never touched a pair before), and waving at Guy and his friends to come up and join her (even though they weren't waving back).

Why don't they come up and join me? she wondered. *Hey—maybe they're shy and geeky now that I'm being so cool.* For some reason she found this outrageously funny and had to stop playing the bongos to go laugh on the shoulder of the lead singer.

Out in the audience Lara made the same face she'd made when complaining about the club's disgusting rest rooms. "She's a *student* of yours?" she asked Sam, as if it were an accusation.

Sam had never seen this side of Josie. But then, he knew high-school students suffered from a great deal of stress and sometimes had to let it out in wild and crazy ways. Sometimes they experimented, exploring the different sides of their personalities, trying to find their true identity. He knew Josie was troubled, and that she was searching for something. . . . He just wasn't quite sure what it was.

He cleared his throat. "She's from Scranton," he said, as if that explained it.

But Josie was too far gone to notice the stares, hear the insults, or realize that she was making a complete fool of herself. All she could feel was the freedom. She tried to get the Rastafarians up onstage to do the macarena with her—they refused, of course; apparently Josie was the only one who hadn't gotten the memo that the macarena had long since gone the way of the twist and the frug.

The lead singer of Ozomatli summed it up for just about everyone when he signaled the bouncer and muttered into the microphone: "Freak."

Somehow Josie was home. It was around one in the morning, and she was talking on the phone to her brother. She was also eating a pie. A whole pie.

"I'm telling you, Rob!" Josie exclaimed. "I think I did it! I'm totally in! I was sooo cool tonight! You'd be so—"

She broke off to stare at the shiny four-pronged utensil in her hand, as if she'd never really looked at it before. "You know what's a weird word? *Fork.*"

She looked closely at her reflection in the shiny surface of the fork, then turned to look at herself on the other side. Wow. That was really strange. She'd never noticed before that if you looked at your reflection on one side, it was upside down. But if you looked at your reflection on the back side, it was right side up. She flipped the fork back and forth several times, studying this strange new discovery. . . .

"Josie?"

Josie dropped the fork and stared at the phone receiver in her other hand. Oh, yeah. Rob . . .

"Wait! Wait! Did I tell you about my new friends?" she gushed. "I made friends with a whole table of Rastafarians. Not one. Not two. A *whole table*!"

Glowing with happiness, still starving, she picked up her fork and dug into the pie.

Clink!

What a minute. . . . Pies don't clink!

She examined the pie plate. It was completely empty. "Oh. My. God. Someone ate my *entire* pie!"

She looked around her kitchen—it was completely deserted. (Or should she say, *desserted*?) Whoever it was, they'd left without saying goodbye.

14

Josie woke up with gentle sunlight streaming across her face and slobber dribbling from the corner of her mouth onto the kitchen table. Her right hand was asleep from where her forehead had been resting on it, squashing it for most of the night. She sat up, shaking the pins and needles from her fingers, not knowing for a moment where she was.

Her eyes fell on the faint purple stamp on the back of her hand—DELLOSER—and it all flooded back into her mind. The whole night, the music, Sam and Lara, the Rastafarians—the *smoke* . . .

Josie coughed. Her throat felt horrible, and her nose felt burned out, as if she'd tried to inhale an entire campfire. Her feet hurt, too, as if she'd been jogging barefoot on gravel. And there was some really disgusting . . . gunk on her shoes.

Her eyes shot to the clock on the opposite wall—8:30. *In the morning!*

Quick—is it a school day?

Uh, uh . . . She counted things out on her fingers.

Yes! Oh, my God. I'm late! Really late!

She grabbed her backpack and keys and dashed out the door. She didn't even take time to look in the mirror or brush her hair.

If she had, she might have seen the purplish letters that overnight had transferred from her stamped hand onto her forehead. They were backward, of course, and not all the letters of the Club Delloser stamp had transferred onto the shiny skin of her forehead.

Only the last five letters.

LOSER. . . .

Josie Geller strode confidently into Southglen South High School, even though she hadn't taken a shower or changed her clothes and was way late. For today she knew she'd entered a new realm of popularity. She rocked Club Delloser with the best of them last night, and today, after two tries at doing the high-school thing, she would finally take her place among the cool kids.

And there they were, gathered around Guy's

locker, dressed cool, standing cool, no doubt talking cool—even smelling cool.

Josie smiled and approached them. "Hi, Guy. Guys. Guy's Guys."

For a moment they all stared at her as if she had a great big zit on her forehead.

And then Guy broke the silence. "Hi, *loser.*"

His entourage burst into laughter, repeating his words "Hi, loser" until they blurred into a raucous chant of "Loo-ser, loo-ser, loo-ser . . ."

Josie stumbled backward in confusion. She was stunned. *No. Not again. What had gone wrong?*

Josie turned to walk away, but the laughter followed her, spreading down the halls like wildfire. She began to hurry, then jog, then run through the gauntlet of kids, who pointed and laughed and shouted, "Loser! Loser! Loser!" as she blindly ran from the pain. . . .

Outside in George's van, Josie's wing-pin minicamera gave him a frantic view of the laughing teenagers as Josie ran, but not what they laughed at. "This cannot be good," he muttered. The kids' faces revolted him. It was enough to make him swear off ever having kids of his own. Damn, teenagers could be cruel.

At last Josie made it to the refuge of the girls' room, and the secret camera on her collar revealed to George that there was no one else in there. That was good. Through the camera's eye, George heard Josie breathing heavily, the sound echoing pitifully off the dingy bathroom tiles. Saw the sink and faucet running water as Josie leaned over and splashed water on her face, saw her trembling hand reach up and yank a paper towel to dry her face. Then George was able to see Josie's face reflected in the mirror.

"Jesus!" he gasped aloud.

There, the purple letters reverse-printed on her forehead read easily, reflected in the mirror: LOSER.

"Oh, man! Look up, girl," George called out, knowing she couldn't hear him. "C'mon—look up!"

But she was too upset. She wiped her mouth, tossed the paper towel into the overflowing trash can, then headed for the door.

George was about to have a heart attack. "FOR GOD'S SAKE, WOMAN—LOOK IN THE MIRROR!"

Something—maybe George's heartfelt psychic vibes—caused Josie to pause with her hand on the door handle. To turn around. To go slowly to the mirror and stare at her reflection. And when she finally saw the purple letters—the word LOSER stamped on her forehead—her hand flew to her mouth in horror, blocking a silent scream.

Agony twisted across her face. And then she bolted into a dented, graffiti-covered stall. . . .

As the tiny wing camera focused on the porcelain bowl, George turned away from the image, whispering a string of oaths at the monsters who could humiliate a sweet girl like Josie so badly it could make her puke her guts out.

Gus's office was dead silent.

Several of the staff had gathered around Gus's TV to watch the latest episode of what some of them jokingly called *Josie's World*. But no one was laughing.

They stared, slack-jawed in shock, at the image and sounds being broadcast from the last stall in the girls' room at Southglen South. Some of the most hard-hearted of the bunch, the crime reporters, the guy who covered the morgue . . . had to turn away.

Gus shook his head. Never in all his life . . . "It's like the All-Humiliation Network," he said in disbelief.

For once, everyone agreed with Gus.

Josie lay curled up in the fetal position on the cold, hard, dingy tile floor, trying to fill her mind with black nothingness. But when she did, images from another nightmare drifted onto the empty stage of her mind.

It's a night of magic, the night of Josie's dreams. She's all dressed up in what she will later realize is a hideous, metallic pink dress, matching gloves, evening bag, and shoes—all of which cost gobs of money, but it was worth it, because she knows this will be the best night of her life, a night she will remember forever. She is going to the prom with the most handsome boy in the world, the most popular boy at school.

Billy Prince.

Nervously she checks her reflection in the blank TV screen and gives her braces another polish with a gloved finger.

The phone rings and she rushes to answer it. "Hey, Billy. . . . Yeah, I'm ready. . . . Sure, I can just wait for you on the front porch. See you in, uhh—a jiffer!"

She hangs up.

Her cute, popular, sixteen-year-old brother Rob comes into the room with his pretty girlfriend on his arm, but for once Josie doesn't feel like the loser in the family. Tonight she has a gorgeous date, too. Tonight she will be as popular as her brother.

Then Josie hurries outside to wait for Billy in the cool spring night. The stars twinkle in the dark sky, and her metallic dress sparkles in the porch light, and she feels pretty and glamorous and . . . special. She is excited and full of the promise of the unexpected and truly feels like a girl in a fairy tale, waiting for her prince.

Then something splendid happens. She sees a long black limousine turn the corner, and then, even more wonderful, it begins to slow down as it nears her house. Oh.

My. God. It's coming for her! She is nearly hopping up and down with excitement. She checks her reflection in the tiny mirror of her compact and dares to believe for the first time in her life that maybe she is just a little pretty, pretty enough to be wanted by the most popular boy in the school. She practices her smile, the smile she will give to Billy . . . along with her heart. She tucks the mirror away and watches the limo come for her.

Should I wait for him to come up to get me? *she wonders.* Or run down to meet him?

The limo cruises to a stop. The sunroof hums open.

And then her date, the beautiful Adonis, the smiling Billy Prince, rises through the opening and waves to her.

Josie waves back and takes a step forward, to run to him, unable to wait.

Then . . . her foot freezes on the second step . . .

As a gorgeous blonde in a dazzling low-cut black dress rises through the sunroof beside Billy.

Josie is confused. Are she and Billy double-dating with another couple? And what are those little things they're holding? Those little white things . . .

Billy and the blonde laugh. Their arms swing back, and then—

Splat!

An egg hits Josie's chest and drips down her shiny metallic dress.

It makes no sense. Josie cannot move. She can only stare down at them as—

Splat!

Another egg hits her in the arm. Another one splatters all over her dress, another one strikes the porch . . .

She holds up her evening bag in a lame defense, too stunned to turn away . . .

"Hey!" Billy Prince shouts at her. "Write a poem about this!"

He rears back and lobs one final egg that smacks Josie in the face, coating her glasses, curtaining off her vision as Billy and the blonde scream with laughter and the limo roars off down the street toward the prom. Without Josie.

All alone, covered in raw egg, legs trembling, Josie collapses onto the steps.

Dreams shattered like eggshells, she sobs into the night.

And the stars call her idiot. Loser. Fool.

15

The Southglen South halls were packed with kids when Josie finally managed to leave the girls' room, barely pulled together enough to aim herself in the direction of the front entrance of the school. She found herself going faster, running now, in her frantic need to escape this sick nightmare, banging into kids, getting whacked by a backpack, sliding on some prom flyer lying on the floor. She slipped, she tripped, she caught her gym shirt and ripped it on someone's protruding protractor (hey, where were the metal-detector guards when *that* weapon came through?), but nothing could stop her till she was out of this horrible torture chamber called high school.

Almost there . . . almost out . . . never coming back . . .

A door appeared where there'd been nothing.

Josie slammed into the solid block of dark brown wood and crumpled to the floor.

Someone had just swung open the big wooden door to the front office. Accident? Or karma?

What did it matter? Josie thought as she lay on the floor fighting the ginger-ale bubbles that swam before her eyes.

Two kids looked down at her.

"Hey—you okay?" one guy asked.

Josie could only nod.

"Wow. You took a pretty big fall," the other one said.

"Yeah," the first one agreed. "Like every loser should."

They laughed, then sauntered off to class.

Josie closed her eyes against the pain. "*As* every loser should," she whispered.

But then she heard another voice, a kinder voice. "Are you okay? Josie—are you okay?"

She opened her eyes to find her brother Rob on his knees, bending over her, stroking her hair back from her face.

"I've been in a horrible accident," she said, rubbing her eyes. "This is a coma-induced nightmare."

"No, Josie," Rob said. "This is real."

She looked up at him, horror in her eyes. "Oh, my God! That's worse!" Then she frowned in confusion. Something was wrong with this picture. "What are you doing here?"

Her brother leaned closer and whispered in her ear, "I just registered." He whipped out his ID—a very good fake ID—to show to her. "Manufactured at the Tiki Post," he said proudly. Then he helped Josie to her feet.

"Are you crazy?" Josie hissed at him. "You can't do this!"

"This is it, Jos! This is my ninth inning! The game isn't over—I just thought it was."

Josie rubbed her aching forehead. All these sports images were really confusing her.

Rob just laughed at her. "Don't you see? I get on the Southglen baseball team, the right scout sees me—I'm into the minors—it's game time!"

"You're twenty-three years old!" Josie exclaimed.

"With the reading comprehension of a fifteen-year-old!" he pointed out. His eyes gleamed. "Plus, I'm popular. . . . You want to be popular. . . ." He patted her shoulder sympathetically. "I can recognize a cry for help when I see one."

"*Hear* one," Josie corrected. "Rob, this is so like you. You know, you can't just come in here and be popular in just one day."

Rob just smiled.

• • •

Three hours and twenty-seven minutes later Josie emerged from the cafeteria line with a trayful of yesterday's reheated glop to hear the cafeteria ringing with the cheer: "ROB, ROB, ROB!"

She spotted her newly registered brother at a center table, an industrial-sized plastic tub of Kole Slaw Food raised over his head, as he consumed the final slurps of slaw. With a roar of victory—Josie hated it when he talked with his mouth full—he slammed the empty container onto the tabletop and raised both fists over his head in a gesture of triumph, a coleslaw mustache embellishing his confident smile.

The entire cafeteria went wild. Josie couldn't believe it! *You'd think he'd just scored the final touchdown at a football game!*

And then, even more astonishing, her brother casually strolled over and sat down—without invitation—at Guy's sacred lunch table.

"Oh, my God," she murmured under her breath. *Now he'll see what it's like. . . .* She watched, breathless, waiting to see her brother get slammed by Guy's elite guard.

Guy turned on him, a crooked smile on his face. Josie waited to see what ruthless barb he'd concocted for her brother. . . .

"Dude, you rock!" Guy gushed.

Josie's mouth hung open in utter disbelief. *No!*

A pretty girl with a killer bod oozed up beside Rob and purred, "Hi, I'm Tracy and I'm sixteen and I'm a gymnast and I don't have a boyfriend."

Rob glanced skyward and mouthed the words, *Thank you!* Then smiled at Tracy. "I'm Rob."

"Duh," Tracy said, imbuing the syllable with more flirtatious double meanings than Marilyn Monroe ever dreamed of.

No, Josie thought. *It's not happening—not twice in one lifetime. Is it simply my karma to forever be outcooled by my baby brother?*

"Hey, where were you last night? I was worried."

Josie could barely take her eyes off Rob sitting at Guy's table long enough to acknowledge that Aldys stood beside her. "What?"

"Last night," Aldys repeated. "Seven-thirty. Na-Na's?" When Josie didn't answer, she explained, "I kept calling you, but I only got your machine. I don't even know your parents' line, and I was really worried."

Josie vaguely remembered her plans with Aldys—it seemed like a lifetime ago. Had that been for last night? Words failed her again, and she fell back on the lame excuse, "Oh, I forgot."

Aldys didn't forgive twice. "Well, maybe you should forget about sitting with us, too."

Before Josie could make up some excuse to smooth things over, Aldys walked off and joined her friends. Josie saw her whisper to them, then watched as the whole table of Denominators looked at her with the same contempt that she usually found in the cool kids' eyes.

Now she wasn't even welcome at the math geeks' table. Now she really was all alone.

Josie's heart was not in the extra laps Ms. Brown found a reason to make her run in gym class that afternoon. When P.E. was over, she lagged behind the other students as they headed back to the locker room.

Hearing cheers, she wandered over to the baseball diamond and somehow wasn't surprised to find her brother at the center of attention. With three men on base, what did her brother do? Hit a single? Choke up? Strike out?

Try a grand slam. A home run with three men on. Four runs with a single whack.

The crowd that had gathered cheered him on as he ran the bases, waving his cap, and when he neared home plate, his fans surrounded him, slapping him high fives, shouting his name. "Rob! Rob! Rob!"

They love him, Josie thought. And she was consumed with jealousy. *How,* how *does he do it?* It was a mystery to which she hadn't the first clue.

She wondered why she didn't hate her brother.

But she didn't. She loved him, just like everybody else seemed to love him instantly. He'd just been born easy to like, she guessed. Maybe you *could* be born under a lucky star. Or under a bad sign, she thought with a sigh.

Back in the girls' locker room, she let her shower run hot, trying to ease some of the misery that seemed to have seeped into her very bones.

She wrapped a towel around herself and scooped up her sweaty gym clothes. When she approached her locker, a group of classmates, already showered and dressed, walked past her, giggling, and Josie imagined that they were laughing at her. *Don't be silly*, she told herself. *People do laugh at other things besides Josie Geller.*

But when she reached her locker, she found it open. And empty. Her clothes were gone.

Her classmates had been laughing at her after all.

Resigned, she tried in vain to smooth the wrinkles out of her sweaty gym clothes before putting them back on.

Five minutes later she shuffled down the hallway in her cheesy green-and-yellow gym clothes smelling like a rank gym shoe. She felt totally beaten. Totally depressed.

The scene at the end of the hall almost put the final nail in her coffin.

Rob looked like a returning hero, a record-breaking baseball player, an astronaut, the guy who'd just won the election by a landslide. Girls clung to him, guys slapped him on the back or punched him affectionately in the arm. Everyone seemed to know his name.

"Hey, Rob!" dozens of friends called.

"Robates, what's up?" someone shouted

"The Rob man. My man Rob."

"Hey, Robbie," Gibby cooed.

"Hey, I am all over your Buick," Kristen gushed.

My Buick, Josie seethed.

She watched as Guy jogged over and shook his hand. "Hey, Robo—how's it going?"

"Nice pants," Rob commented, nodding his head the way cool guys did. "They are rufus."

I'm gonna hurl, Josie thought, turning her head—

Only to spot, down the hall, a huge banner streaming across the hallway that read:

IMPEACH SYDNEY ANAKOWSKI
ELECT ROB STUDENT BODY PRESIDENT

"Hey, Rob, see you at the carnival later?" a girl called in a giggly voice.

"It's Robilicious!" someone squealed.

Josie felt faint and leaned her forehead against the wall. Paper crinkled against her skin—she'd leaned against a notice of some kind. She looked at the notice cross-eyed, but one word still leaped out at her: Rob.

She rubbed her eyes and looked again.

FINAL CAST LIST FOR HAMLET

HAMLET: ROB

She couldn't believe it. It was happening all over again.

16

Garish-colored lights mocked the stars, calliope music snaked and curled its way into every crevice, and shrieking people clung to giant whirling metal wheels that plagiarized the rotations of the universe.

Or at least, that's how the carnival looked to Josie—a grotesque parody of life.

Why did people love to pay money to get on rides to scare themselves silly when life was already scary enough on its own?

She wandered under a cheery banner that read SOUTHGLEN HIGH SENIOR NIGHT, feeling nauseated by the smells of greasy food, trampled hay, and oily, grinding gears. She'd always liked carnivals and fairs, but tonight, all alone, she could see only the grime behind its tawdry bogus come-on.

Why am I here? she moaned to herself.

Because your job depends on it.

Maybe it was time to check into what Welfare had to offer. Check the Web site for the Foreign Legion.

Up ahead she saw the Denominators clustered like orange baby chicks around some cheesy midway game. As Josie drew closer, she saw that they had their calculators out and were engrossed in trying to guess how many jelly beans there were in a huge glass jar. *What a great use for all that brainpower,* she thought. But . . . it did look like fun. Aldys hadn't spoken to her since that day in the cafeteria. Would she if Josie joined them now? She raised her hand in a greeting, but they didn't notice her—or chose not to. She felt invisible.

She wandered on until she came to the giant illuminated circle of the Ferris wheel, and suddenly she wanted to ride it, to have it gather her up and carry her high into the sky, away from everything on the ground.

She got in line and waited.

Up at the front of the line Guy and his friends were being boors, as usual.

"This has been so much fun!" Kristen gushed. "We've been first in line for every ride."

"That's 'cause we cut every line." Tommy guffawed.

When the wheel stopped and the dark-haired, muscled carny opened the gates, everyone rushed on, piling into the hanging baskets, two by two. When Josie finally reached the gate, there was one empty car left. She climbed into it alone.

The carny held the safety gate open, waiting expectantly. When Josie looked at him questioningly, he said, "Where's your partner?"

"I don't—I don't have one," she mumbled, looking down into her lap.

The carny turned toward the crowd and, cupping his greasy hand to his mouth, barked out, "I GOT A LONELY RIDE IN BUCKET SEVEN! SINGLE!"

"Do you have to yell like that?" Josie hissed.

In the basket just above and behind her, she heard Guy's buddy Tommy jeer, "Of course, it's Loser holding up the ride!"

Josie lowered her eyes, her cheeks burning. *I should be used to this kind of trash talk by now, should let it roll right off my back.* But she wasn't, and she let it hurt her. Did anyone ever get used to it?

"This seat taken?"

Josie's eyes flew open. Sam Coulson smiled at her, his hand on the safety bar. She couldn't contain her smile. Did he realize he was rescuing her from humiliation? She glanced behind him. No sign of Lara. Maybe she didn't like Ferris wheels.

Whatever the reason for his arrival, she sighed in relief and welcomed him by scooting over to make room. "Thank you."

He climbed in, the carny fastened the safety bar, and the ride jerked into motion.

"Whoa!" Sam said nervously.

Josie laughed with him. But as their seat glided backward, gathered speed, and began to rise in the air, she saw her favorite teacher clutching the iron safety bar as if he were trying to bend the bar with his bare hands.

"Are you—scared?" she whispered.

Sam Coulson cleared his throat. "I'm gonna tell you something here, and I hope it doesn't undermine my position as an authority figure."

She waited politely.

"I'm a little afraid of heights."

"You're afraid of the Ferris wheel?"

"Actually," he said with a grin, "it's more the plunging headfirst into the crowd part that gets me."

"I bet you'd feel better with that Gordie Howe helmet on, huh?"

He turned to her with a look that tore at her heartstrings. "Hey," he said softly, clearly touched. "You remember that story?"

"Of course. I remember everything from your class."

They smiled at each other, and Josie felt gravity

loosen its grasp on her. They could have been the only two people at the fair.

But the moment was interrupted by their bucket swaying dramatically. Josie glanced up. Tommy was seriously rocking his bucket ahead of them. She noticed that her teacher looked a little green as they crested the top of the ride and began to fall to earth.

"Yooooow," Sam said, under his breath.

Josie laid a hand on his and told him, "Don't look down."

But they were plunging toward the ground. "Out of my control," he replied, as his eyes stared at the very thing that frightened him. Tommy was still goofing off, rocking his seat, which jostled the one Josie and Sam were in.

At last Sam kind of lost it and shouted, "TOMMY! CUT IT OUT! ENOUGH!"

Tommy stopped.

Sam cleared his throat, shifted in his seat, and, finally, turned to look at Josie with a slightly embarrassed smile. "I said that as a chaperon."

Josie laughed, and Sam seemed to relax. Then the Ferris wheel bottomed out and began its slow ascent again.

"Okay," he said, reassuring himself. "This is okay. Smooth."

Josie smiled at him again—she'd been doing a lot of that since he climbed aboard the ride with her. And then her heart melted when she realized that the Ferris wheel terrified him. Which meant he never would have chosen to ride it on his own.

He'd climbed aboard the ride to rescue her.

She closed her eyes to hide the feeling she wouldn't allow herself to name as it sang through her heart.

"Can I ask you something?" Sam asked her.

Anything.

"Do you think I tell too many stories in class?"

"That's what makes you interesting," Josie murmured; then quickly added, "As a *teacher.*"

"God, I would love to think I'm an interesting teacher," he said, looking up across the sky now, no longer fixated on the ground. "I mean, I had maybe one or two teachers in high school who had any passion at all."

"You do. Seem to. Have passion." Josie's mouth felt dry. "In the classroom," she added.

He chuckled. "You have to say that. You're my student."

"I don't have to say that."

Their eyes locked as the Ferris wheel carried them into the starry sky. Josie's heart soared.

A jolt from the bucket ahead of them sent their seat rocking again.

"If the bucket's a-rockin', don't come a-knockin'!" Tommy hooted.

Josie and Sam laughed uncomfortably, shifting in their seats.

Sam cleared his throat. "Boys."

"I know," Josie said.

Sam ran a hand through his dark hair and grinned crookedly. "I'd like to tell you that we all grow out of it, but that's a lie. Some of us will always be rattling cages."

"Why do you do that?" Josie asked.

Sam seemed taken aback by the seriousness of her question. "I don't know," he said honestly. "And you know what's scary—when you get older, it just gets more confusing." For a moment, he stared out at the lights of the carnival spread out below them like a jeweled carpet, his mind on other things. "Lara—my girlfriend you met at the club? We've been going out for five years. She wants me to move to New York," he revealed.

Josie's heart skipped a beat. She reminded herself she couldn't lose what wasn't hers to keep.

"And I should do it. Make the commitment. Grow up," Sam went on, sounding as if he were trying to convince himself. "I mean, I know we have our differences—our tastes in music, she hates sports, and I hate antiquing in Connecticut. But . . . you know, five years, it's a long time."

The Ferris wheel neared the bottom of its rotation, and Sam suddenly seemed to realize that he was talking—a lot—and that Josie hadn't spoken.

"You know what, I shouldn't be talking about this stuff with you."

"That's okay," she told him. "It's nice to have someone to talk to—"

Tommy rocked their bucket again, and Sam gripped the safety bar. "Same here," he said through clenched teeth.

Suddenly they stopped rocking.

In fact, the entire Ferris wheel ground to a stop with the two of them swaying gently at the very top.

Sam's eyes were shut tight, and Josie looked down.

It was okay. They'd stopped to begin letting people off.

Sam realized it, too, and let out a breath. Then he looked over at Josie. "All I can tell you," he said softly, "is that when you're my age, the guys will be lined up around the block for you."

Josie suddenly felt shy. "You have to say that. You're my teacher."

"I shouldn't say that," he said, "*because* I'm your teacher."

Their smiles faded as they sat there alone together, far above the rest of the world, and realized they weren't in danger of falling head over heels to the ground. They were in danger of falling head over heels in love.

Then the Ferris wheel jerked, carrying them back to earth.

When they reached the ground, Sam jumped out and reached for Josie's hand to help her down. "Thanks, Josie. That wasn't as bad as I thought."

"When are you going to open your eyes?"

"I'm thinking when I'm home."

17

Southglen South's fabulously popular new student—and already star player on the top-ranked baseball team—sprawled in the dugout with a bunch of other players, appreciating how wonderful life was. Sunshine, good friends, and baseball—what more could a guy want?

A few dates wouldn't hurt, but everybody's favorite guy didn't want for those, either.

High school. It was even better the second time around. Especially when your name was Rob.

"Hey, Rob," his teammate Packer said, "thanks for showing me that new grip. It totally changed my swing."

"No problem, man," Rob replied generously.

They traded one of those elaborate, fraternity-like handshakes to remind themselves they were brothers in cool.

Then a wisp of a cloud marred the beautiful day.

Josie.

Rob caught sight of her walking across the field. Head down. Feet dragging. All alone.

Like a rich man at a table of plenty gazing at the poor and the hungry, he choked on the taste of his success.

He'd never quite understood what the deal was with Josie. Rob loved his big sister. She had triple the brains he had, and he knew deep down she was a real sweetheart. Why did the popularity that came so easy for him elude her so?

It was one of life's puzzles.

He smiled, remembering how she'd always let him tag along with her when he was little. How she took up for him when he got into scrapes with Mom and Dad. How she'd read to him to help keep him from scratching when they both had chicken pox when she was six and he was four. How she gave him a boost into the tree house when his arms wouldn't reach.

She'd been a pretty good big sister all in all, he realized. A sister who had kept on believing in him—even when he'd given up on himself. So what if she corrected his grammar all the time? He wouldn't trade her for the world.

Maybe now he had a chance to give her a boost, too.

"Hey," he said casually, "you guys know that girl Josie Geller?"

"You mean 'Loser'?" Matz said, and looked around for confirmation. Several of the guys laughed.

"No, dude—*Josie*," Rob said, as if he thought they'd misunderstood who he was talking about. "We used to go out. . . ." He paused to reel them in a little.

As a team, the guys leaned forward.

Rob shrugged, a look of manly regret on his face. "She dumped me. But we're still good friends. And she is *amazing*—if you know what I mean."

The guys all looked at one another, stunned at this unbelievable news. Rob and the Loser? It . . . couldn't be.

But the Rob man had spoken.

The Southglen South High School baseball team sat up in the dugout and gave Josie Geller a second look.

In biology class the next day, Rob got a second opportunity to give his big sister a plug.

He and Gibby and some of the other cool girls were examining the classroom's life-size skeleton, which some of the kids had nicknamed Kate. They were supposed to be identifying the various bones to fill in on a worksheet. But Gibby couldn't stop staring at the skeleton's narrow waist.

"All right," Gibby said, "that's it. Just water and Ex-Lax till prom."

"Hey—Josie's dad invented that stuff," Rob interjected. Rob grinned—he was pretty proud of that one. Thought it up on the spur of the moment.

The girls murmured various exclamations of shock and disbelief.

"No, really," Rob insisted. "Josie's like the heiress to the Ex-Lax fortune."

"Shut up," Kristen said, totally impressed.

"Yeah, she's loaded," Rob said, thinking, *what would really ring the gong with these girls?* Oh, yeah. Perfect. "She spends all her vacations on the family yacht in the south of France."

No, it can't be, they thought.

Josie Geller—on a yacht? In France, the coolest of the cool countries in the world?

But if Robbie said it, it had to be true.

And the door to their clique opened just a crack.

Later, behind the bleachers, Rob let only his best buddies in on the most amazing tidbit of all.

"No way," Tommy gasped.

Rob nodded.

"She used to date the drummer for the Big Bad Voodoo Daddys?" Jason cried.

Rob nodded.

"No way," Guy said, then sighed wistfully. "I

always wanted to be a drummer. . . ."

Rob was really enjoying this priceless bit of fabrication. Hey, maybe Josie wasn't the only writer in the family. "Yeah, well," he embellished, "she left *him* for the drummer from Sister Hazel."

"Rufus!" Guy exclaimed.

Bingo! Rob had a feeling his big sister's whole life was about to change for the better.

Josie went through the cafeteria line, filling her tray with sugar, grease, caffeine, and chocolate. She paid, grabbed a straw, then stepped out into the lions' den known as the cafeteria.

Strange, Aldys was walking toward her. And she was smiling.

"Hey, Josie," she said. "Listen—I'm really sorry I snapped at you the other day." She shrugged toward the Denominator table. "Do you wanna—"

"Oh, Aldys, you know . . ." She'd really like nothing better than to go sit with someone who might have no interest in humiliating her. But then she looked past Aldys at her brother Rob, who was sitting at "the Table"—where Kristen, Guy, and some of the other cool kids usually sat.

He was waving at her.

Hesitantly, she waved back.

He shook his head and started waving again—waving at her to come over and sit down.

No. She shook her head. *I couldn't.*

He glared at her and pointed at her, then at the empty seat. *Now,* he mouthed.

"Uh, Aldys," Josie said distractedly, "I have to . . ." She shrugged and walked timidly over to Guy's table, leaving Aldys staring at her in disbelief.

Rob rewarded her with a lazy smile and stuffed a french fry in his mouth. But he didn't say a word.

Josie laid her tray on the table and sat down.

"Hey, Josie," Gibby said. "It's Josie, right?"

Josie nodded.

Kirsten leaned across the table and smiled. "Can I just say—I totally love Ex-Lax."

"O-kaaay," said Josie, eyeing her brother suspiciously. "That's good to know."

"I can't believe you dated Big Bad Voodoo Daddy," Tommy burst out.

Josie shot her baby brother an are-you-out-of-your-mind? look.

"Hey," Rob said seriously, "I told you—Josie doesn't like to talk about that."

"Yeah, Tommy," Kirsten said. "That's totally *go-chay.*"

"I think it's pronounced *gauche,*" Gibby said.

"Yeah, it's French," Josie said, glad for once that she had something to contribute to the conversation. "There's no accent aigue, so the *e* is soft."

Everyone stared at her. The table was totally silent.

I totally blew it, Josie thought.

"Duh, of course you would know that," Gibby said at last, laughing. "From being on your yacht in the south of France."

Now everyone smiled at her. Josie was floored.

She glanced at her brother and almost laughed at his smug smile. *Like, do you owe me or what?* it said.

She couldn't believe it. Her brother had done the impossible—made a place for her at the Cool Table; everything on Life's menu was available to her now. Before she could stop herself, she winked at him. *Yeah, I owe you.*

The others at the table didn't miss a second of this unspoken dialogue. Kristen, Kirsten, and Gibby exchanged knowing smiles.

Maybe, just maybe, they thought, there was still something going on between these two. . . .

18

Sam Coulson, English teacher, inexplicably found himself standing in the front of the biology classroom as juniors and seniors filed into the room for the annual safe-sex lecture.

Most of the teachers went to extreme lengths to avoid being within a wing of this room when S-E-X was the topic, so this year the emcee duties had fallen into his, er, lap.

He glanced around the room to avoid too much eye contact with the students, who were already suffering from fits of the giggles. The walls had been papered with public-service announcement posters. Neat little stacks of pamphlets about AIDS and sexually transmitted diseases had been laid out on the front desk, next to plastic, cross-section, biology models of the male and female reproductive organs. That alone was likely to encourage some kids to behave.

He glanced at the wall clock, then double-checked the time on his watch. If the speaker didn't show up soon, he might be giving the talk himself.

Just the thought of it made him blush.

But he'd do it if he had to. The subject was too important—and the students were too important to him—not to give them the straight scoop.

He glanced at his watch again. He sure hoped the speaker showed up soon.

Josie came into the classroom with some of her new friends, tried not to look Sam Coulson in the eye, and frowned when she wound up in one of the front desks. *She* certainly didn't need this talk at her age, and she would have preferred to sit in the back and give some of her classmates front-row seats to the show.

She stared at the posters, her desktop, the floor, to avoid looking at Sam. But she glanced up when she heard a tiny tapping sound. Glancing up from her desk, her eyes widened when she spotted Anita—*Anita? From the Sun-Times?*—waving wildly from the other side of the glass door.

Josie shook her head. Anita just smiled and waved.

Josie frantically waved her hands, trying to tell

her, "Get out of here!" Anita frowned and mouthed, *Say what?*

Good Lord. Didn't the woman ever play charades?

Josie waved one more time—and noticed Sam Coulson staring at her. She quickly put her hands in her lap and sank down in her seat, but Sam followed her gaze. Looking incredibly relieved, he strode to the door and opened it.

"Hi," he said softly. "You're here for the sex talk?"

"Well," Anita said, smiling in surprise, "I like a man who gets to the point."

"You're Pam?" Sam said.

Anita's hand slid to her hip, and she purred, "If you say so."

With a nod, he ushered her into the room, stopping when they stood in front of the class. "Welcome, juniors and seniors," the teacher said. "This is Pam Kitterman. She's our district health counselor, and she's here to lead our sex discussion."

"I am?" Anita exclaimed. She looked at the room of expectant faces and shrugged. *Sure, why not?* Who was more qualified than she? "Oh, I am. Hi. Okay. Sex. Yes, well, sex. What's to say, really, y'know? You like a guy, you do it. Sometimes he calls. Sometimes he doesn't."

Sitting right in front of her, Josie was absolutely mortified.

Anita leaned over to Josie and whispered, "Hi!"

"What are you doing here?" Josie whispered back.

"I had a lunch break, so I thought I'd come by and see you." She glanced back over her shoulder. "Your teacher is a fox!" Then she stood up and, in a normal voice, said, "Why don't we discuss that after class? But the burning is totally normal." She checked her watch. "Oh, look. Class is over already." She took a step toward the door—

"I thought this was a forty-five-minute seminar," Sam said.

"Right," Anita said. She turned around and faced the class. "Right."

She walked back to the front of the classroom. "Okay, sex. Let's see. . . . Sex is really fun."

Josie shot her a killer look.

"*When* you're old enough," Anita amended. "Which none of you are, trust me, I should know, 'cuz when you lose it to some guy named Junior with really bad breath in the back of a van at a Guns 'n' Roses concert, you're gonna wish you listened to your mom when she said, 'Y'know, no one's gonna want to buy the whole dang ice-cream truck when you're handing out the Popsicles for free.'"

There was a deafening silence.

No one had ever, *ever* said anything like that at one of these seminars.

Sam would have said something, but he couldn't get any sound to come out of his throat.

"Okay." Anita folded her arms and smiled at the class. "Any questions?"

Josie relaxed then. Nothing that followed could be worse than that opening speech.

Sam relaxed a little, too. He guessed he had to admire the instructor's straight-talking style with the kids. It was probably more effective than the typical talk. But he figured the rest of the lecture would be a little less . . . sensational.

But that was before the hands-on practice with the condoms and the bananas.

Anita walked among the desks, really getting into her role now. "Okay, I know it's hard."

The group tittered.

"*Difficult,*" Anita amended. "But safe sex is really important. I try to practice it every day."

Josie nearly choked.

Kristen, Kirsten, and Gibby were sitting together a few seats away, more interested in Josie than in bananas. "Wait, rewind," Kristen said. "Do you really think she hooked up with our Rob? They're so . . . different."

"Sometimes opposites attract," Gibby pointed out.

"Yeah," Kirsten agreed. "Look at Bert and Ernie."

Anita happened to look up then and see a

woman through the window of the door. She was holding a model of the uterus and waving. *Uh-oh. It's the real Miss Kitterman!* she thought. Without missing a beat, Anita strode to the door, locked it, and pulled down the shade. She was having too much fun to stop!

Tracy, sitting next to Josie, struggled to follow the instructions. "God, I can't do this," she said.

"Maybe because we're not supposed to be having sex with bananas," Josie said.

"You know what, though?" She leaned in closer to Josie and confided, "I feel like I'm really ready to do it. To have sex for the first time."

"Wow," Josie said. She wasn't sure she wanted to be the one this young girl confided in. "That's big," she said. "I mean sex is a really big deal. You shouldn't do it until you know you've found the right person."

Josie didn't know Sam was listening.

"You know, Adélie penguins pick one mate," Josie told Tracy as they practiced. "They spend their whole lives looking for that one other penguin, and when they find it, they know. That's the penguin they stay with for the rest of their lives."

Tracy frowned. "But I'm not a penguin."

"It's an analogy," Sam said.

Josie jumped at the sound of his voice and let go of the small item she was trying to slip over the banana—and it flew off, hitting her teacher in the face.

Josie turned to Tracy. "Excuse me. I have to die now."

Fortunately for Josie, the intercom came on with a news bulletin from the student body president. Josie wondered if the girl ever went to class or simply hung around in the office.

"Hey, guys—Sydney again! Don't forget—no going into the library 'cuz of that little asbestos problem. And about prom—"

Hands froze on bananas as the room went dead silent.

"Really bad news," Sydney moaned. "We just got the word from intelligence—Eastglen High . . . "

Everyone leaned toward the intercom speaker.

". . . is doing the millennium theme for prom, too!"

Chaos reigned at Southglen South. People screamed. People cried. One girl fainted. Sera squeezed her banana so hard it oozed out of its skin. Other kids beat their bananas against their desktops. Brett, totally stunned, peeled his banana and began to eat it.

"All right, guys, let's calm down," Sam Coulson called out over the tempest. "Calm down."

No one paid attention.

"SIT!" he shouted.

Everyone sat, even Anita.

"Now look," Sam said calmly. "Let's focus. Prom theme. We need a new idea." He looked out across the sea of miserable faces, hoping they might exhibit greater creativity here than they did as a rule in English class.

"Oh! How about 'Under the Sea'?" Anita suggested brightly.

The class booed.

Anita looked insulted. "Well, excuse me."

"What about the Roaring Twenties?" Sam suggested. "Or the eighties?"

The class groaned.

"What do you think we are?" Gibby said huffily. "Amateurs?"

"Josie," Guy said.

Sera frowned. "That's not a theme."

"No," Guy said, shaking his head. He turned to Josie, newest addition to the realm of the social elite. Heiress. Yacht owner. Babe so fluent in French she could differentiate between accent aigue and accent grave. "*Josie* will have the answer," Guy pronounced.

A hush fell across the classroom.

Josie felt their expectant faces turn to her like sunflowers to the sun.

Josie shuddered. Where was Rob when she really needed him?

She looked at Tracy. "How about . . ." But her mind—as it so often was when a whole roomful of people stared at her—was a total blank. What had been the theme at her own prom—the one she'd never made it to? It was so fantastic . . . she couldn't even recall.

She looked around the room, searching for something, anything in the room that might inspire her. . . . The safe-sex posters and anatomical models weren't quite the feeling she was looking for. *What about* . . . and her eyes Velcroed with Sam Coulson's expectant, encouraging brown ones.

"How about . . . 'Meant for Each Other,'" she murmured, "famous couples throughout history?"

The room was as silent as a morgue as her classmates considered it. Josie held her breath . . . it seemed like for hours.

And then Guy smiled. "Yeah, that's it."

Instantly the rest of the room rocked with delight over the perfect idea.

"Yeah!" someone shouted out.

"That's so romantic," a girl cooed.

"Rufus!" someone pronounced—the *Good Housekeeping* Seal of Approval.

Josie soaked up the approval like a dried-up sponge. Was it the first time in her life that she'd suggested something that was branded cool? It overwhelmed her, the rush it gave her, and she made several little half bows as she murmured, "Thanks. Thank you."

And then her eyes sought the approval of one who was way past the age of caring about prom themes. . . .

Sam was smiling at her.

So was Anita.

And so was the perfect Guy Perkins.

19

Josie watched as the old MILLENIUM banner was torn down and a fresh banner that read MEANT FOR EACH OTHER was hung its place. She felt as if this were the most important day in her life. She was legit. Kosher. Sanctioned, validated, and authenticated. Her prom idea—and she—had been formally accepted.

Her euphoria went beyond the knowledge that she'd saved her job and might now actually get the story she'd been sent to high school to uncover. For the first time in her life she was experiencing what it felt like to be cool.

And cool meant accepted.

Cool meant loved.

Now everything changed.

Instead of wandering the school alone, bumping into locker doors and getting jostled, she and her popular girlfriends—Kristen, Kirsten, and Gibby—cut a wide swath when they walked through the halls. The crowds parted for them like the Red Sea before Moses. Her friends even dug up pins that matched her little winged hidden camera. She had a primo seat at the center of the action in the cafeteria. And the name Loser . . . everyone seemed to have forgotten the word was ever spoken in the same sentence with the name Josie Geller. The club fiasco? Never happened. When she went home at night, she didn't cry into her ice cream alone. When she woke up in the morning, she looked forward to going to school.

Josie was happy. Happier than she'd been since . . . well, since the day she'd been hired by the *Sun-Times*.

Josie's coworkers at the *Sun-Times* were happy, too—if they got their daily fix of *Josie Goes to High School*. Conferences, lunch dates, interviews with inside sources . . . everything was now rearranged around Josie's schedule. Gus couldn't remember when he'd had an office to himself.

The staff seemed particularly interested in the romantic story line.

Josie and her English teacher falling all over

each other as they painted a romantic backdrop of a sunset for the prom . . .

Josie and her English teacher in his classroom, their fingertips touching as they went through a deejay's case of CDs, picking music for the prom . . .

Josie and her English teacher having a one-on-one discussion about the love poetry of Shakespeare while the rest of the class planned their costumes for the prom . . .

Josie and her new friends perched like birds in the bleachers one afternoon, sunning themselves in colorful bikini tops and shorts as the baseball team practiced down on the field. In the stands nearby, Guy played something cool on his guitar.

Josie raised her face to the sun and let the warm rays seep into her bones. She felt as if she'd been plucked from a dark movie theater and thrust onto the screen, to play the starring role in the movie she'd once only watched from the back row. It all seemed a little unreal still.

"Josie," Gibby said, "you have totally transitioned."

"Transitioned?"

"You crossed over," Gibby explained.

"Into our group," Kristen added. "It's really hard to do. Some kids try for all of high school and never make it."

"Wanna-bes," Gibby said distastefully. "Kirsten," she added with a proud smile, "transitioned last year."

"Her dad sold a car to Leonardo DiCaprio's uncle," Kristen revealed, "and before he picked it up, her dad let us all sit in it and take pictures."

Wow, Josie thought. *Now, that was pretty darn cool.*

Gibby starting giggling then, nudging Kristen in the ribs, exchanging glances with Kirsten.

Josie looked down through her sunglasses at the ball field to see who'd made the big play.

But the action the girls were interested in wasn't down in the dirt. It was up there in the bleachers, where Guy had targeted Josie as the object of his total attention.

"Guy is totally crunching on you," Gibby gushed.

Josie glanced at him through her sunglasses but tried not to move her head so she wouldn't look as if she were looking. "Do I want to be crunched?"

"By Guy?" Gibby gasped.

Gibby, Kristen, and Kirsten were unanimous in their answer: "Oh, *yeah.*"

A slow grin spread across Josie's face. It might be fun to be crunched for once.

Down on the infield a bat cracked and the ball shot for left field, a base hit for the other team for sure—

Thonk! Till the shortstop leaped up and snatched it right out of the air.

A shortstop by the name of Rob.

Rob's team whooped and hollered as Coach Romano ran out of the dugout and slapped Rob on the back. "Great playing, Rob!" he exclaimed. "You might be just what Southglen South needs to get to Nationals."

"You mean—I'm playing in the championship game?" Rob said, afraid to believe what he was hearing.

"Playing?" Coach Romano shook his head. "You're starting shortstop. And I don't mean to put more pressure on you, but there are going to be some pro scouts there—"

"Oh, man!" Rob couldn't contain his delight. He grabbed Coach Romano in a bear hug, which made the coach a little uncomfortable. But when Rob let go, Coach gave Rob a slap on the behind as the happy shortstop headed for the dugout.

Josie dashed to squeeze onto the elevator at the *Sun-Times*. The doors closed on her huge backpack, and she really had to scrunch to pull it inside enough to let the doors close. She heard some grumbling at the back, but she was almost late for a staff meeting, and if she waited for the next elevator, she'd be late for sure.

With her tousled blond hair, majorly cool teen clothes, and slouch, Josie stood out among the tired, dull-eyed employees like a sunflower in a field of dried-up weeds.

She stared at the door in front of her nose as she waited for the elevator to carry her to her floor. She normally rode elevators in silence, without looking at anybody, but today she felt someone's eyes on her. She glanced sideways.

A young woman gazed at her as if she were a rock star.

"I really loved you in the sex-ed scene," she gushed.

Josie nearly dropped her gum—especially when she heard a murmur of agreement ripple through the crowd behind her.

When the elevator stopped, Josie spilled out and raced through the bullpen.

As she did she passed Merkin Burns, office assistant, seemingly glued to the phone.

"No way . . ." he said into the receiver. "Yeah?. . . No way."

Without breaking stride, Josie snatched the phone out of his hand and hung it up, then proceeded to the conference room. She knew Merkin must be staring at her; good, she'd wanted to do that for nearly a year.

She knew she'd reached the conference room when an older woman ran out crying.

Uh-oh, meeting's already started, she realized. *Better hustle.*

Josie slipped into the conference room. Rigfort presided at the head of the table like God. The staff around the table looked stunned—business as usual.

"Alrighty then," Rigfort belted out, glancing down at the paper on the table before him. "Next on the agenda—sack races at the company picnic—yes or no?"

As quietly as possible, Josie tried to make her way through the crowded room to the only empty seat, whacking some of her coworkers with her huge backpack as she went. Josie the copy editor was normally nearly invisible, but today Josie the teenager seemed to be attracting lots of attention. "Sorry," she whispered. "Hi." When she felt Rigfort's eyes on her, too, she mumbled, "Sorry I'm late."

Her backpack thumped the floor as she sank into a chair next to Anita.

Anita leaned over and whispered "I *love* that jacket!"

"Thanks!" Josie mouthed with a smile.

"Miss Geller!" God boomed.

Josie straightened up in her chair and tried to look serious.

Rigfort leaned forward expectantly, his hands clasped before him on the conference table.

"What's the status of your story?"

"Oh, it's great," Josie said with great enthusiasm. "*Totally* rufus."

Gus and Anita exchanged a puzzled look. *Rufus*? they mouthed. At least a half a dozen reporters made a note to look up the unfamiliar word the copy editor had used as soon as they got back to their desks.

Rigfort continued to stare at her expectantly.

I guess he wants a little more detail, she decided. She dragged her backpack into her lap and dumped everything out on the table. Nearly every item advertised to a teenager in the last six months spilled out across the polished wood—notebooks, CDs, scrunchies, a hacky sack, purple-glitter nail polish. . . . "I have, um . . . notes here somewhere. . . ." She rifled through the junk, then exclaimed, "*There's* my math homework!" She smoothed the crumpled paper out on the table.

"Geller!" Rigfort bellowed. "I don't need your notes. I need your *story*! Though I speak for everyone when I say I've seen the tapes, and it's compelling stuff."

Josie squirmed in her seat; it was hard to think about her whole day being monitored by her coworkers.

"But I want a story in two weeks," Rigfort demanded. "I'm saving the 'Life and Style' cover for you." He smiled a rare smile—though it looked a little like the smile of a crocodile. "You're gonna make one hell of a reporter!"

Josie blushed in delight at the rare compliment. He'd said it, right here in front of everybody! She couldn't believe how perfectly her life was going.

"Oh, and if you don't," Rigfort tossed off casually, "you and Gus are fired."

Josie gulped and shared a look of horror with Gus.

"Now, on to the next order of business," Rigfort said, ruffling papers. "Marketing department—yes or no?"

20

When Josie pulled Bambi into her parents' driveway that night, beer cans and teen-agers littered the lawn. Josie shook her head. Just like back in high school, the minute her parents left town, Rob threw an Instant Party.

The front door opened, spilling music, light, and people out onto the sidewalk. Josie wedged herself into the crowd, then slowly wriggled her way through the bodies toward the back of the house. People called out her name and she waved—a nice change from being ignored or asked to leave.

She found her brother Rob in the kitchen, mixing margaritas and wearing . . . a huge sombrero? No, it couldn't be. Not Ms. Knox's sombrero! Josie acknowledged that she was in the presence of a master. Only Rob could wear the humiliation hat and make it look cool.

Josie smiled at her friend Tracy, who sat on the counter, gazing with total adoration at everything Rob did.

"Hey, Rob," Josie said, "what's going on?"

Tracy giggled. "I'm Rob's prom date!" she announced, as if she'd just won the lottery.

"Really?" She smiled at Tracy but glared at her brother as she pulled him aside. "Rob, that girl is sixteen!" she hissed.

"And a *gymnast*!" Rob added, as if *he* had just won the lottery.

"She's sixteen years old, Rob," Josie repeated, wondering which was interfering with his brain more: the sombrero or the margaritas. "That's totally and completely illegal."

Josie felt an arm snake around her shoulders. "Hey there." It was Guy.

"Hey," Josie said. "There."

Guy captured her hand and began to lead her out of the kitchen. "Come here," he said. "I want to ask you something."

"See you around the cellblock, Mrs. Robinson," Rob quipped as they went away.

Josie glared at her brother as she left the room. Low blow—the mother who seduced the college-age Dustin Hoffman in *The Graduate* was at least forty!

Rob salted two wide shallow glasses, filled them with margaritas, and handed one to the exceedingly lovely and flexible Tracy.

Grinning, she clinked glasses with him, then took a sip. "What do you want to be when you grow up, Rob?"

"Well," Rob said honestly, "a ballplayer."

"No, I know," Tracy said. "But what if you don't make it?"

Rob shrugged and chugged his frozen drink.

"I mean, you don't want to be working at a mail place the rest of your life," Tracy went on. "It's okay for an after-school job, but, come on—'Hi, I'm Rob, and I run the Tiki Post'? Totally lame." She started to giggle.

Rob didn't. That was exactly what he had been doing. He'd thought it was okay—hey, mail packaging was an important part of the modern economy.

Now. . . He was getting an ice-cream headache from his frozen margarita. Or maybe it was her drunken snobbish laughter that gave him the chill.

Now this is awkward, Josie was thinking. She was at a party with a cool guy who was beginning to have that I-wanna-make-out look in his eyes. The party was at the home of Rob, whom she supposedly had dated. And now her guy, Guy, had led her to an upstairs bedroom in Rob's house—awkward enough on its own. But this bedroom door just happened to have an old bicycle license plate nailed to it. A license plate that said JOSIE. That was because the room was her old bedroom.

So, like, how was she supposed to explain why she had a bedroom in Rob's house?

"Maybe we should go in a different room?" she suggested, trying to drape her body in a way to hide the name.

Guy shook his head. "I already checked. There are some pretty serious couples in there." He reached for the doorknob and opened it for her, the perfect gentleman. Josie's feet took her inside. Inside, they'd be okay.

Josie spotted all her old spelling-bee trophies etched with her name on them lined up on a shelf. She knew she should have taken them with her to her apartment. She pretended to be browsing the room and tried to appear nonchalant as she turned trophies so the names didn't show. Without the name, the room was just any average girl's room.

She watched, curious, as Guy eyed the trophies, the stuffed animals, the many sets of encyclopedias. This was her room, her private sanctuary, where she'd studied, and dreamed, and cried. It still looked much the same way it had when she was really in high school. How would Guy react? Would he get a sense of who she was by exploring her private world?

Guy let loose a low whistle. "Rob's sister must be such a *loser*."

Josie felt the air rush out of her. There was that word again. *Loser*. *Josie Grossie* updated for the late nineties.

Beneath the mantle of her newfound popularity, Josie shuddered.

Then Guy sat on the bed. "Come here," he said. "Sit down."

He smiled at her, and that was when she noticed the framed photo on her nightstand—a nice family photo of Josie with Rob and her parents.

Josie dived across the bed to turn it facedown on the table, then smiled back at him, as if crash-diving onto a bed with a handsome teenager boy sitting on it was something she did every day. Instead of never.

Guy acted almost shy. "I'm sure you've probably heard that I want to ask you, but I'd like to know if you'd go to the prom with me. I know we didn't hit it off right at the beginning, but—"

"Yes. I'll go. Yes," Josie said.

Guy leaned in as if to kiss her, and whispered, "Rufus." Then he pulled away. "But I don't even know where you live."

"You know what?" Josie said. "Why don't you just pick me up here? We could all share a limo."

"Cool." Some guys started calling his name,

looking for him downstairs, so he stood up. "I'll catch you later."

When she was sure he was gone, Josie flopped back on her bed, and stuffed animals fell all around her.

She was going to the prom with the most popular guy in school. It wasn't a joke! And this time nothing could go wrong.

21

The next day Josie and Rob walked confidently through the hallway. Kids greeted and high-fived them both.

"Hey, Jos. Hey, Robster," Jason said.

"Looking good, guys," Brett said.

"Hey, Jos," Tommy called out. "Rob—rufus kegger!"

Cool parties with no grown-ups around—it was still a total status-maker.

When they turned the corner, Josie whispered to her brother, "Rob, this is unbelievable." She shoved through the double doors leading into the gym. The place was a flurry of activity, a staging area for the prom. Various committees were set up at tables throughout the room. "I spent my whole life wanting to fit in, and now—"

Gibby and Kirsten ran up to Josie. "Hey, Josie—who did Archie date—Betty or Veronica?"

"Betty," Josie replied without having to think about it.

"Told you!" Gibby said. She and Kirsten went off together to work on some decorations.

Rob spotted Tracy and made a beeline for the gymnast.

"I always liked Betty better."

Josie smiled at the sound of Sam Coulson's voice and turned around. "You did?"

Together they walked through the prom props, as if they were on a romantic date—through the flowers, past the bistro table, by the backdrop of the sunset. Sam picked a flower and held it out. "Oh, yeah. Betty was so spunky and fun. Veronica may have had great legs, but she was too moody. Very high-maintenance."

Josie laughed.

At the ticket table Aldys and Tommy were arguing.

"You can't *refuse* to sell me a ticket to the prom," she was telling him.

"Listen, *Alpo*," Tommy said, "we can do whatever we want."

"Oh, I get it," Aldys said, ignoring the cruel play

on her name. "It's that pesky making-change part that's confusing you guys. Here. I'll make it easy. Money—" She dropped bills on the table and snatched a ticket. "Ticket." She stalked off before he could make any more snide remarks.

Kristen walked up to Tommy and began to whisper.

Sera ran up to Josie to ask, "Were Tweedledum and Tweedledee a couple?"

Sam and Josie shared a look.

"Well, in a strict sense," Josie answered, "probably not. But for prom—sure."

"Thanks!" Sera said, and ran off.

"You're really doing a great job here, Josie," Sam told her. "I like your can-do attitude."

"Thanks," Josie said shyly. "They weren't related to Humpty Dumpty, were they? Tweedledum and Tweedledee."

"Probably distant cousins," Sam said. "They did have that egg shape in common."

"But Humpty Dumpty was alone."

"That's sad, isn't it?" Sam said. "He had to sit on that wall all by himself. He deserved to have somebody."

"That's really what we all need, right? Someone to sit up on the wall with us to watch the world go by."

"To put us back together when we fall."

They'd moved closer without realizing it.

"Do you think you'll find her?" Josie breathed.

"Yeah, actually I do," Sam said.

Lost in each other, they leaned closer still. As if they might kiss. . . .

"Oh, my God!" Sam said, suddenly breaking the spell. "I almost forgot—I got you a meeting with the admissions guy from Dartmouth!"

"What?" Josie exclaimed. "But—I wasn't even going to go to college—"

"No, I know, but I pulled some strings, got him to look at your writing, and he agreed to meet you."

"Oh, yikes!" Josie said. Meeting with a college admissions official, going over school records—this was a masquerade she couldn't pull off.

"I told him, 'If I'm wrong about this girl, you can take away my teaching certificate.'"

"Wow," Josie said breathlessly. "You believe in me that much."

Sam took her hand. He looked into her eyes, meaning every word. "Of course I do. Josie, you owe it to yourself—to your writing—to go to college. You're a *great* writer. You just have to find your story. . . ."

• • •

"*That's* your story."

It was later that day, and Josie sat in Gus's office at the *Sun-Times*, staring at her boss's TV, which had just rerun that very private romantic moment as if it were an instant coffee commercial.

Josie didn't understand what Gus was getting at. Then slowly it began to dawn on her. "You're crazy," Josie said. "I can't—I can't—no. *No*."

Gus rolled his eyes. "It's got it all—sex, intrigue, immorality in the education system—"

"He's my teacher!" Josie protested.

"That's the best part!" Gus exclaimed. He pictured the headline. "Teacher-Student Relations: How Close Is Too Close?" He rubbed his hands together in gleeful anticipation of a hot story. "We're gonna blow the lid off it!"

Josie jumped to her feet. "There is no lid! Nothing's going on between Sam and me."

Gus's eyebrow shot up at the familiar use of her teacher's first name.

"Coulson," she said. "Mr. Sam Coulson and me."

"Not yet," Gus said. "But every person in this office comes in here and watches you guys! It's like the goddamn *Young and the Restless*! Rigfort's *salivating* over it."

"You already pitched this to Rigfort?!" Josie exclaimed.

Gus leaned toward her, all business. "Josie, this isn't a joke. You heard Rigfort. It's both of our asses on the line. *This* is your story."

Josie wished she'd never learned to write.

22

Prom night arrived at last.

Getting ready for the prom—it was one of the great nights of a teenage girl's life.

Only Josie wasn't a teenager, she wasn't really a high-school student, and her prom date was research for a major news story she had to come up with in less than two weeks.

She sat in her bathrobe in front of her dressing-table mirror and stared at her clean face. *I'm an undercover reporter in a Halloween costume,* she reminded herself.

But her heart beat faster, ignoring the argument. She wasn't just pretending tonight, wasn't just acting. She was living it. She was doing what thousands of people probably wished they had the chance to do—to live their high-school years over, to have one more chance to rewrite the story, to edit out the dangling modifiers and misplaced verbs. To live it again—and maybe this time get it right.

So she had a job to do, too. Who said she couldn't do it and still have a marvelous time?

She raked her makeup-strewn dresser top searching for the eye shadow she'd bought at the last minute, a glimmery creme to make her eyes shine. Not that she needed it—her eyes were already shining. But then her fingertips fell upon her tiny flight wings pin. The secret minicamera that reported everything she said or did—reported everything those around her said or did—to the entire staff of the *Sun-Times*.

She picked up the pin in the palm of her hands and examined it. It really didn't go with her outfit, nor did it fit her mood; pinned to the Elizabethan gown she'd chosen to wear, the airplane wings would be a complete anachronism and intrude on a special night that she longed not to share.

She wished that, for one night, she didn't have to wear the pin.

When Josie arrived at her parents' house that evening, she found her brother wearing a white dress shirt, a pair of white boxers, and black socks.

He'd better hurry, she thought, or he'd be late.

Rob stopped in the middle of filling two flasks and whistled at his sister. Shyly Josie whirled around, showing off her full-length Elizabethan costume, then waited expectantly for his response.

"Wow, Josie," Rob said, "you look really . . . "

"Rufus?" Josie said hopefully.

"Yes." Rob grinned. "Exactly. *Major* rufus."

"Thanks!" Josie gushed. Then she frowned at her half-dressed brother. "And you are—?"

"Duh, Josie." He struck a pose. When she still shook her head, Rob put on a pair of black Wayfarer sunglasses, got a running start, then skated sideways in his socks across the polished wood floor.

"Tom Cruise! *Risky Business*!" he exclaimed.

Josie laughed. *The knucklehead . . . if ever a guy was born to be in high school,* she thought with affection, *Rob was the one*. And lucky for her he'd held open the door. "Rob . . . thanks. For everything." She took a deep breath, trembling with excitement. "This is really happening! I never thought—"

"I know," Rob said.

The grin they shared held years of unspoken affection.

Then Rob dashed off to add "the garnish" to his costume—drugstore aftershave.

Josie checked the clock on the mantel, then nervously checked her reflection in the TV screen, just as she had eight years before. The braces were gone, the hair was blonder. But had she really changed?

She took a deep breath; it was time.

Lifting her long skirts, Josie hurried out the front door to wait for Guy in the cool spring night. The stars twinkled in the dark sky, and the golden threads in her Elizabethan gown sparkled in the porch light. Like millions of girls on prom night before her—and like the millions who would most certainly come after her—she felt her heart overflowing with excitement, with the promise of the unexpected.

And for a moment she allowed herself to believe that she was pretty. Pretty enough to go to the prom with the most popular boy in school.

A long black limo rounded the corner, just as it had eight years before. And instead of delight, Josie felt a wave of unexpected nausea wash over her.

She froze when she saw the sunroof glide open.

Felt terror snake up her spine when she saw Guy rise through the opening, holding something white—

No! It was happening all over again, just as it had eight years ago, just as it had with Billy Prince.

Josie didn't wait for a blonde to pop up beside him. She panicked. She ducked . . .

And then she saw the roses.

Roses?

No eggs. No blonde. No horrible insults hurled through the night to shatter her heart.

Only a handsome young man dressed in romantic Elizabethan garb, holding out a dozen white roses to her from the sunroof of a limousine.

"Come on, beautiful," Guy called up to her with an irresistible smile. "What are you waiting for?"

Nothing, Josie told herself. *It's already here.*

With a whoop of joy, she ran down the steps in her Elizabethan gown to change history.

23

The ride in the limousine was so cool; Guy was at his charming best, and Josie felt like a princess from a fairy tale as they leaned back in the plush seats and wished on stars through the sunroof. When the limousine pulled up to the curb at the country club, the stars seemed to have fallen to earth. Thousands of tiny lights twinkled in the trees. Music danced through the air. Above the building Josie's words—MEANT FOR EACH OTHER—flashed on and off in neon lights. How many writers ever got to see that?

As Guy came around to open her door, Josie marveled at her high-school friends, magically transformed by costumes into people of mystery and romance. Anthony and Cleopatra. Superman and Lois. Lewis and Clark.

Josie spotted Sera in a rabbit suit, waving to her lagging date, who was dressed as a tortoise.

"Hel-lo!" Sera called to him. "If you don't hurry up, we're gonna miss the whole thing!" Apparently Sera, not so gifted in the classroom, had a real talent for casting.

As soon as Guy helped her from the limo and watched it drive away, three more limos drove up and discharged their passengers. A guy and a girl stepped out of each one. But all three girls were wearing identical straight blond wigs and extremely short, tight dresses.

Gibby, Kirsten, and Kristen stared at one another in horror.

"Oh. My. God!" Gibby cried. "You *totally* ripped off my Malibu Barbie idea!"

"Uh-uh!" Kristen said. "I'm Disco Barbie!"

"And I'm Evening Gown Barbie," Kirsten said.

"Right," Gibby said, eyeing Kirsten's short tight miniskirt. "That's not an evening gown."

"It is on Barbie," Kirsten said.

Then the girls spotted Josie and Guy and ran over, squealing about their costumes.

"Josie, you look so rufus!" Kristen exclaimed.

"Yeah," Kirsten said. "Who are you guys?"

"Please don't tell me you're Medieval Barbie," Gibby begged.

Josie laughed and shook her head. She was so

proud of her idea, she wondered if she could get Sam—Mr. Coulson—to give her and Guy extra credit in English. "Rosalind and Orlando," she told them.

The three Barbies frowned.

"From *As You Like It*?" she hinted.

Their blank stares made them look like real Barbies.

"Shakespeare?"

The silence was embarrassing.

"Look!" Guy interjected at last. "I get to have a sword!"

The three Barbies got that, and *ooh*ed and *ahh*ed and admired his sword.

Guy escorted Josie inside, where the club looked even more beautiful. Lights sparkled off ice sculptures and champagne fountains spouting nonalcoholic punch. The buffet table looked as if it could feed thousands.

Josie noticed two older gentlemen in tuxedos. They carried clipboards and wore buttons that said NATIONAL PROM JUDGE.

A month ago Josie couldn't have cared less about the competition for best prom theme. But tonight it suddenly seemed to matter, especially since it was her theme.

The two men contemplated one of the ice sculptures on a buffet table. "It's deft and unique without being derivative," said one.

"Hey!" the other one said, glancing down the table. "Pigs in blankets!" Forgetting the sculpture, he bolted for the tiny cafeteria snack cum hors-d'oeuvre.

Josie and Guy moved toward a table surrounded by cool kids. She couldn't help but remember the night at Club Delloser, when she'd gone to take a seat and they'd closed her out. Tonight they scooted around to make room.

Josie sat down and noticed that Kirsten was making weird faces. "Kirsten, what are you doing?" she said.

"I'm practicing my surprised face for when we get named to prom court," she said.

"Okay," Josie said under her breath.

"You having fun?" Guy asked, slipping an arm around her shoulder.

Josie smiled at her date. She'd been a little rough on Guy in the beginning. But now that she'd gotten to know him, she had to admit he was really sweet. He was the kind of date she would have killed for when she'd gone through high school the first time.

"Oh, yeah," she answered, gazing with pleasure at the fantasy world whirling around her. "The best."

• • •

"This is the most beautiful prom I have ever been to," Anita gushed.

She—and half the *Sun-Times* staff—had crammed into Gus's office to watch the prom. The hidden camera on Josie's wings pin fed the action to George, who was watching with a date in the comfort of his dimly lit news van, which fed the image to the monitor in Gus's office.

Anita had a front-row seat. Gus pretended to work on something on his desk, but kept a furtive eye on what was happening.

Cynthia hurried in with a huge bowl of microwave popcorn. "Did I miss the crowning?"

"No, but I'm closing the pool in five minutes." Merkin held out a bowl filled with cash. "Josie's odds are three to one. For prom court, two to one. And even odds the kid sticks himself with the sword by the end of the night."

Cynthia tossed in her cash and squeezed into the front row so she wouldn't miss a thing.

Popeye and Olive Oyl had just boogied onto the dance floor, where Sonny and Cher, Jack and Jackie, and the Blues Brothers were getting down.

Risky Business Rob was trying to dance with Tracy, dressed as the Rebecca DeMornay character, who was too drunk to walk, much less dance. "Are you havin' f-f-f-fun?" she asked.

"Yeah, definitely," Rob said, holding her up.

"Good." Tracy hiccuped. "Gibby gave me champagne."

"Maybe we should sit," Rob said. He slipped her arm around his shoulder and helped her to a couple of chairs by the side of the dance floor.

Tracy wobbled in her seat a moment, then gave him a serious look. "Rob, I've—I've thought about it a lot. And I think—I mean, I know. You're the one. My penguin."

That was certainly a new way of putting it.

Rob looked at her. She was young. She was beautiful. She was tipsy.

And she was trying to put her legs behind her head.

Rob didn't quite know what to make of the situation. "Wow—I . . . "

"Rob, I mean it," Tracy insisted. "I want you to be my first. Me and you." She stared at the floor, clutching her stomach as her head rolled around on her shoulders. "Once the floor stops spinning"—she hiccuped—"let's have sex."

Is this every prom guy's dream or what? Rob thought.

But then he looked around the room at the party raging on. This was a high-school prom. Some skinny kid was getting beat up in a corner. A couple of kids were sneaking smokes. And a few couples up front appeared to be holding a hickey contest.

Twenty-three-year-old Rob felt like a time traveler.

I can't do this, he realized.

He gazed at Tracy—she was a really sweet kid. She deserved to fall in love the first time with another sweet kid.

"I'm gonna get you some water," he told her. "And then I think we should get back out on that dance floor and boogie."

Rob got up, kissed her tenderly on the top of her head, and headed for the refreshment table.

Tracy, one leg still around her head in an amazing demonstration of gymnastics skill, hiccuped, then fell backward off her chair.

Over at the cool table Gibby's face contorted with a look of pure horror. But she was no longer practicing how to act surprised when they announced prom court. She was really horrified. "You guys," she said. "What is the one thing that could ruin my senior prom?"

"That you'd trip on your Barbie heels and I'd get named prom queen?" Kristen said, quickly covering her mouth. "Whoa. Did I say that out loud?"

Then her eyes fell upon the truly upsetting event that had Gibby's knickers in a twist.

Aldys and the Denominators had appeared at the entrance of the country club. And they didn't just come in quietly and skulk around the edges of the cool crowd. They came in two at a time, linked with ropes, forming a human ladder. As Kristen, Kirsten, and Gibby watched, their faces contorted into silent screams, the Denominators crossed right through the middle of the dance floor, interrupting everything with their unwieldy, tied-together conga line.

They stopped at the Cool Table.

"So what you supposed to be?" Gibby snapped. "Other than freaks?"

Aldys wasn't fazed by the sneer in Gibby's voice. "We're DNA. A double helix. But I guess you'd know that if you'd actually passed bio."

Kristen's face bore the horrified but strangely fascinated expression of someone ogling a wreck on the highway. She reached out and touched the rope binding Aldys to another girl, whose name she'd never bothered to learn.

The girl slapped her hand. "Please don't touch the hydrogen. It's rented."

Halfway through the evening Guy's charming handsome face faded into oblivion as Josie's eyes fell upon another face. The face of Sam Coulson.

He'd climbed to the stage at the front of the dance floor and was fiddling with the microphone, trying to adjust the height.

Sam Coulson could even make the manipulation of sound equipment look sexy.

Josie's eyes returned to her date, and she tried to tell herself their eight-year age difference was not really that great.

Yeah, right, she thought. *Ten years ago I could have been his baby-sitter.*

Sam's voice riveted her attention to the stage. "Well, the moment has arrived," he said cheerfully, holding up an index card. "Our 1999 prom court!"

The crowd on the dance floor surged toward the stage and fell utterly silent.

"The princesses are . . . Miss Kristen Davis, Miss Kirsten Leosis, and Miss Gibby Zarefsky. And the princes are Mr. Thomas Salamey, Mr. Jason Way, and Mr. Rob—"

Sam looked at the card and frowned. He flipped it over, then looked around the audience. Nobody could help him. Nobody knew Rob's last name.

"Mr. Rob . . . *Mr. Rob*!"

The crowd erupted in cheers and whistles and screams.

Gibby, Kirsten, and Kristen all jumped in preplanned delight—it looked like a Barbie commercial.

Rob seemed genuinely surprised and followed Jason as he whooped and hollered and carried Tommy up to the stage piggyback. Gibby kept making her strange look-of-surprise faces as she and the other two new prom princesses made their way to the stage. When they had slipped their prom-court sashes over the costumes and waved to the crowd, Sam looked to the card again.

"Next up, Southglen's prom king—"

Guy was already halfway to the stage, trading high fives with guys in the crowd, accepting kisses from the girls . . .

"Guy Perkins!" Sam revealed—unnecessarily.

The crowd went wild. Guy reached the stage and took his crown and scepter.

"And this year's prom queen . . ." Sam began. He looked at the card.

He looked at Josie. . . .

Who tried not to read what his eyes were saying . . .

While Anita, in the *Sun-Times* office, squeezed her eyes shut and crossed her fingers on both hands and prayed for the win . . . .

"Ladies and gentlemen . . . "

The room got so quiet, you could hear crepe paper curl.

Sam smiled and shouted, "Josie Geller!"

The celebration on the dance floor rivaled the election-night crowd of an upset candidate.

At the *Sun-Times* Anita leaped to her feet, knocking over Cynthia's popcorn. Cynthia didn't care because she was jumping up and down, too.

"Yes!" Anita screamed. "You go, girl! Yes! Yes!" She danced around the room, then threw her arms around Gus in a monster hug. Gus was shocked—but didn't protest.

Merkin dolefully began to hand out cash to the winners of the office pool.

In the news van George's date threw her arms around him and kissed him beneath the sparkling lights of his disco ball.

Back at the country club, Josie felt powerless to move, yet somehow found herself on the stage waiting to be crowned prom queen by the most handsome man in the world. She had to be dreaming. It was too wonderful to be true.

Grinning with delight, Sam placed the queen's tiara on Josie's head and slipped a bouquet of flowers into her trembling hands. As their fingertips touched, they locked eyes for a moment . . .

Then Sam cleared his throat, remembering where he was—and who he was. "And now, as is custom, the king and queen will have their first dance." Reluctantly he turned Josie over to Guy.

Guy led Josie onto the dance floor and swept her into his arms for a slow dance. As Josie leaned into his strong embrace, whirling in a spotlight before the crowd, the world seemed a glittering and wonderful place.

"Hey, what are you thinking about?" Guy whispered into her ear.

"Shakespeare," Josie instantly replied. "How he described a night like this: 'Look how the floor of heaven is thick inlaid with patinas of bright gold.'"

Josie sighed; then asked, "What about you? What are you thinking about?"

Guy smiled. "My sword."

Something like a switch flicked on in Josie's brain. "Oh."

"Josie," Guy murmured, missing the tone in her voice, "you rock my world. You're like the most amazing girl I've ever dated. You're so smart and fun and crazy! You rock my world!"

"You said that already," Josie remarked.

After the dance Josie excused herself to go get some punch. Her mouth seemed to have gone suddenly dry. Guy easily found entertainment in the admiration of some of his friends.

Josie stood by the buffet, hoping the *Sun-Times* staff were drooling over the food, wondering why she felt let down all of a sudden. Maybe a breath of fresh air would help. She turned suddenly and found herself face-to-face with Sam.

"Josie," Sam whispered, "you make a really beautiful prom queen."

"Thanks," Josie murmured. "So do you."

They both laughed, embarrassed, at Josie's flub.

"I always feel like such a goofball in these penguin suits," Sam said, pulling at the lapel of his tuxedo. "Like I'm at my own wedding or something."

For some reason that made them both blush.

Sam cleared his throat and rocked on his heels. "You wanna . . ." He gestured toward the dance floor.

Josie nodded shyly. "Yeah, okay."

Sam took her by the hand and led her into the dance.

Across the floor Guy shyly walked up to Aldys.

She immediately went on the defensive, but Guy held up his hands in a show of truce.

"Hey, listen—it's prom," he said. "How about we let all the old shit go. Would you like to dance?"

His smile was so charming, his eyes so warm and open.

Aldys did what most unpopular girls do when the most popular guy asks them to dance. She let a tiny smile escape, flattered.

"If," Gus teased, "it's okay with the rest of the double helix."

Aldys laughed and allowed herself to be swayed. With a shrug she hoped costumed her delight, she untied herself from the rest of the Denominators and slipped her hand into his.

Out on the dance floor Josie relaxed into Sam's

embrace. Josie wondered what Sam was thinking. He wasn't wearing a sword.

"Proms always make me sad," Sam murmured, as if in answer to her thoughts. "They're so final. Graduation. Everyone's scattering, moving on."

Josie found herself asking, "Is your girlfriend here?"

"No," Sam said, his voice a mere whisper. "I'm alone."

Josie's heart pounded in her ears, and she heard herself ramble, "It's weird, because *prom* is actually from the word *promenade,* and it's not really a 'promenade,' is it?"

She looked up into his eyes, and the feelings she couldn't hide behind her nervous chatter shone in her eyes.

Sam heard what she was really saying, and smiled. "You're amazing, Josie Geller."

Across the room Gibby/Barbie winked to her Barbie friends and pulled a can of dog food out of her purse. Alpo dog food.

Jason grinned and pulled out the can opener he just happened to be carrying in the pants pocket of his tuxedo. "Allow me." He opened the can with a dramatic flourish, then passed it to Kristen.

Kristen held her nose and made gagging sounds, then, giggling, handed it off to Tommy.

Tommy hid the opened can behind his back. Then he searched the dance floor, hoping for a glimpse of that one special girl. . . .

Ah, yes. There she was, dancing with Guy.

The lovely Aldys.

Yeah—*not*.

"Hang on to her, bud," Tommy muttered beneath his breath. "'Cause it's time to feed the dog."

"Have you thought any more about Dartmouth?" Sam asked Josie.

"Yeah, I have," she said. But this time, when she looked up into his eyes, and lost herself in the feelings she saw simmering there, she experienced an epiphany: a sudden perception of an essential truth.

She would never utter another false word to Sam Coulson.

Slowly, surreptitiously, her hand wandered to her bodice, where it covered the wings that concealed the hidden camera. With deft fingers she slid the pin from the fabric, then let it quietly fall to the floor.

Her lips trembled a little as she smiled up at Sam. "There's something I have to tell you . . . "

A minuscule crunch beneath her heel told her that she had permanently shut down the *Sun-Times* electronic peephole into the *Life and Loves of Josie Geller*.

• • •

"What the—?" George interrupted his make-out session in the *Sun-Times* surveillance van to jump to his feet, banging his head on the spinning disco light. He pounded the side of the snowy TV monitor, but it was no use.

Prom Cam had gone on the fritz.

The spellbound audience in the *Sun-Times* office uttered a collective *gasp*.

"Tell him what?" Cynthia shouted at the blank, hissing TV screen. "Tell him *what?"*

Sam Coulson looked deep into Josie Geller's eyes. "There's something I have to tell you, too. . . ."

Josie started to say she wanted to go first. . . when something over his shoulder caught her eye.

Dog food.

Josie tried to ignore it and tell Sam—

Wait a minute. Dog food?

Josie stared over Sam's shoulder.

A can of dog food—in Tommy's hand. . . .

Raised high above Aldys's head.

Completely unaware, dancing in Guy's arms, Aldys spotted Josie staring and smiled at her.

And Josie saw herself, eight years before, as if a home video were playing in her head. . . .

• • •

She is on the porch outside her house—watching the handsome Billy Prince and his beautiful blond date laugh at her as egg drips down her face. . . . The pain and humiliation is unbearable. She wants to do something, fight back, but she is unable to move. . . .

"Nooooooooooo!"

Josie moved without thinking of the consequences.

She tore herself from Sam's arms and lunged for Aldys, trying to save her friend, and herself, and every other poor girl who ever had her heart trampled by a cruel, conceited jerk.

Stumbling in her long skirts, she crashed into Aldys and pulled her down to the floor.

Tommy lost his balance and his grip on the can.

The thick, chunky dog food spilled anyway.

All down the front of Guy's Elizabethan shirt.

24

The music stopped.

Everyone stared.

The only sound in the room was the rattle of the dog-food can as it rolled across the dance floor.

Until Guy groaned at the mess and turned on Josie. "*What* is your problem!" he shouted at her, his voice echoing in the silent room.

"I knew it!" Gibby chimed in. "You *are* a loser."

"You ruined the whole thing!" Kristen cried.

"You do not deserve to be prom queen," Kirsten declared.

No one said a word. This was pretty new territory. People occasionally transitioned into the cool group. But no one had ever seen someone so publicly and so humiliatingly thrown out.

Josie looked around at all the faces, all the staring eyes, the kids who didn't know what to think on their own until it had been validated by others they recognized as cool. She watched them as they huddled in the safety of the masses, thankful that *they* weren't the ones being publicly humiliated.

Josie should have felt horrible. But she didn't.

She felt strong. Strong because she knew what she thought. Strong because she had something powerful to say.

"Let me tell you something," Josie said quietly.

Nobody moved.

Josie took a deep breath, then said, "I don't care about being the prom queen."

She saw shock on some of their faces. *Just wait till they hear the rest.*

"I am twenty-five years old."

Josie saw every possible emotion play out on the faces of the crowd. Shock. Revulsion. Disbelief.

She found her brother in the crowd. Risky Rob did not look pleased. She shook her head at him, hoping he'd understand why she had to end the masquerade.

The next part was going to be really tough, but she knew she had to say it. "I'm here as an undercover reporter for the *Sun-Times,* for God's sake," she continued.

The shock on Sam Coulson's face was tough to

handle. This was not the way she had wanted to tell him. But she couldn't change that now, and she had to trust that he'd understand.

"And," she went on, "I've been beating my brains out trying to impress you." She tore off her crown and tossed it to the ground.

Kristen ran out and scooped up the dented tiara like a stray dog going after a scrap. It was disgusting.

"I want to tell you something," Josie said. "You people—Guy, Gibby, the rest of you—who have been keeping the geeks down through the ages. You will spend your lives trying to figure out ways to keep others down, because it makes you feel more important. And you will miss out on so much."

She nodded at Aldys, who stood silent, clutching her arms to her chest. "Why her, huh? What did she ever do to you?"

No one answered, of course. Guy and his friends didn't even have the grace to hang their heads.

"Let me tell you something about this girl," Josie said. "She is unbelievable. I was new here, and she befriended me, no questions asked. But you people," she said to Guy and his crowd, "you were my friends only after my brother Rob posed as a student and told you to like me."

Rob looked mortified, and Josie hoped that he'd be able to forgive her.

"But y'know—I have to thank you. I got to go to an amazing prom. I got to be prom queen. I got to be cool. It felt good." She shook her head. "But not as good as being myself."

She paused again to let that sink in. To let it sink in to her mind as well.

"And to *all* of you, there's a big world out there. Bigger than prom. Bigger than high school. When you get there, it won't matter if you were prom queen or the quarterback or the biggest nerd in school. What matters is that you don't regret who you were, who you are. What if Steven Spielberg had quit the audiovisual club because it wasn't 'cool'? What if Rosie O'Donnell had stopped cracking jokes because someone told her they were stupid? What if Michael Jordan never went back to basketball after he got cut from his high-school team?"

Josie gazed at the silent faces. Were they listening to her? Did her words mean anything at all?

"In this room right now, there could be a future Nobel Prize winner, a Supreme Court Justice, an amazing mom. Find out who you are and don't be afraid of it."

It was advice she needed to take herself.

She looked around the room, searching for the one person whose reaction to everything she'd just said really mattered to her. For Sam. But she couldn't find his face anywhere in the crowd. Perhaps he'd gone outside.

"Now if you'll excuse me," she said quietly, "I have some business to take care of."

As she moved out of the spotlight, she heard someone—maybe Sonny or Cher?—holler, "Right on!"

The words seemed to release the PAUSE button. The kids began to clap and holler and whoop for her. A sense of freedom filled the room as the music began again and couples flooded the dance floor—even the kids who'd previously just hugged the walls, afraid they'd make fools of themselves. The Denominators led their own conga line.

The judges were so moved by Josie's speech they were in tears.

"This prom had it all," sniffed Judge No. 1. "Laughter, tears, an amazing climax."

Judge No. 2 couldn't speak, he was so overcome. He just gave it two thumbs up.

Josie smiled as she reached the front doors. Maybe they had listened after all.

As Josie pushed out into the cool night air, searching for Sam, she allowed herself to hope that now, maybe, he and she could . . . what? Start over, perhaps, free to share whatever feelings they had for each other, and see what might happen from there.

She searched the porches, the yard, the parking lot for Sam, but saw only shadows.

Footsteps made her turn, but it wasn't Sam. It was George from the *Sun-Times* news van. "The feed's down!" he gasped, as he ran up to her. "Gus is going ape shit! Did you get a story? *Please* tell me you got something on Coulson!"

At the mention of his name the teacher stepped from the shadows. The look on his face told Josie he'd heard.

"So—surprise!" Josie said lamely.

Sam shook his head in disbelief and walked off. Gathering her skirts, Josie ran after him.

He turned back and faced her. "'Surprise,' you were doing a story on me?"

"No! Surprise, I thought you'd be—"

"What?" Sam said. "Happy? Why? Because it turns out all along that I was allowed to be attracted to you?"

"You were attracted to me?"

"Goddammit, Josie! Drop the act. Do you know what I was going to tell you in there?"

She shook her head.

"That I decided to break up with Lara and *stay in Chicago*."

He raked a hand through his hair and turned away from her. "What the hell was I doing? Thinking I could be in love with a *seventeen*-year-old . . ."

"I was going to tell you about—"

"You set me up," he said. "For a *story*." He shook his head, as if to clear it. "I can't believe I considered waiting for you."

He was going to wait for her? Wait for her to grow up? Oh, God. That was just about the sweetest thing she had ever heard. She laid a hand on his arm and smiled. "But now you don't *have* to wait."

"Now I don't *want* to!" he bellowed. "I bought all of your penguin crap. I thought I found her—the right one! And the problem was she was too young! No—" he corrected himself. "The problem was, she didn't even exist!"

"*But I did exist!*" Josie exclaimed. "I *do* exist. I'm the same person!"

Sam shook his head, his eyes cold and hard. "The person I cared about wouldn't have done this. Everything out of your mouth has been a complete lie. I don't know *you* at all. For all I know," he said ominously, "you could *hate* Dorothy Parker."

"But I don't!" Josie cried. "Look," she said more softly, trying to reason with him, "you could get to know me—again."

Sam glared at her, then turned to walk away.

"Please," Josie pleaded. "Please don't walk away."

But he wouldn't even turn around. "I just can't look at you the same way."

Then he got into his car, the engine roared to life, and he sped out into the night.

Josie rode around for a while in Bambi, unable to find her direction. When she finally made it back to her apartment, she found Rob slumped in her doorway, still in his *Risky Business* shirt and underwear, his sunglasses shoved up on his forehead.

"Josie, finally," he said. "I just wanted to come over and make sure you're okay."

"Really?" she said, surprised and touched by his kindness.

He pulled himself to his feet and glared at her. "No—*not* really, Josie!" he shouted. "NOT REALLY!" He rubbed his face with both hands, trying to control his anger. "How could you do that to me?" he demanded. "I *helped* you. I got you everything you wanted. And how do you repay me—you blow everything TWO DAYS before pro scouts come to see me play. Once they had seen me really play, they wouldn't have given a damn about my age."

"I wasn't even thinking about—"

"No," Rob said. "You weren't."

Josie didn't know what to say. It didn't help that her brother looked as miserable as she felt.

"Don't you realize," he said, "the only time I was *really* happy in the last five years was when I was playing ball with those guys?"

"I—"

"No, shut up, Josie. Just shut up." And he stormed off.

Stunned, Josie fiddled her key into the lock and shoved her way into her apartment.

It had turned out to be a night to remember after all.

25

The next morning Josie was summoned to Gus's office. As she sat down in the chair before his desk, she couldn't help thinking how much it felt like the principal's office.

Gus slapped a newspaper down on his desk and growled.

It was not just any newspaper. It was the *Chicago Tribune*—the *Sun-Times'* biggest rival.

And it had Josie's photo on the cover.

Josie leaned forward to read the headline:

REPORTER REVEALED AT
LOCAL HIGH SCHOOL

Ouch. She picked up the newspaper and began to read. It was a terrible story. First of all, there was a comma splice in the first paragraph. Then there was an incorrect verb tense in paragraph two. Three misspelled words and counting. And worst of all, they spelled *Josie* with a *y*.

"Your story was Rigfort's baby," Gus said. "We were scooped! We've got nothing. Zippo. You totally and completely screwed both of us."

"Maybe I could talk to Rigfort," Josie said, trying to calm her boss down. "You know, tell him the whole story."

"I'll tell you a story," Gus barked, glaring at her across the desktop. "It's about this shy copy editor who makes a mockery of herself and her boss when she completely botches her first assignment as a reporter."

Two months ago Josie would have crumpled beneath his harsh words, then scampered back to her office to cry behind closed doors.

Not anymore.

She stood up and slammed the newspaper onto Gus's desk. "We are not screwed. Yes, I made a mistake. But we *will* have a story." And in that instant the story came to her. She knew what she would write. A story no one would be able to forget. She nodded, smiling. "You will have an *amazing* story."

She stormed out of the office, and as she marched through the bullpen, Anita fell into step with her.

"Josie—Josie! How'd it go? Did he ream you?"

"Yeah, but I'm okay," Josie said. "I've got some work to do."

"You need my help?" Anita asked.

"No, thanks. I'm doing this on my own."

As she walked past Merkin's desk, she held out her hand. "Merkin. Hi-Liter."

Merkin slapped a Hi-Liter into her hand like a nurse slapping a scalpel into a doctor's hand.

Anita watched her friend proceed to the elevator, something new in her step, in the set of her shoulders. So the *Josie Geller Show* on Gus's television had been canceled. Anita had a feeling the next episode was about to unfold right under their noses.

Josie went back to high school. But things were really different this time. She wore a smart tailored pantsuit and carried a briefcase. She took the steps to the front entrance two at a time. Nobody hid her car. Nobody called her a loser. Because this time she knew exactly where she was going.

As she strode purposefully down the hallway, the kids stopped and stared at her. But this time she barely noticed.

Then she rounded a corner and came face-to-face with the ever-popular Guy. He didn't seem so sure of himself now.

But she smiled at him; he'd been such a big part of her life here. She felt an odd sort of affection for him, like a faded memory of a boyfriend who would always be young in your mind even though you had grown older.

But now Guy was the nervous one. He dropped his notebook, and papers scattered across the floor. Josie bent to help him pick them up.

"Uh, hey, umm—Ms. Geller? This is totally embarrassing, but my mom, she's all worried about me getting a job after graduation. She wanted me to ask you about, like, an internship for me, at the *Sun-Times*?"

It really hit her then. Guy wasn't a major threat in the universe; he didn't have all the answers; he was just a seventeen-year-old kid after all.

"I'll do what I can," she promised. "And tell your mom not to worry—you'll do okay."

Guy looked immensely relieved.

With a sigh she continued down the hall till she reached her real destination—the guys' locker room at the gym.

"WOMAN COMING THROUGH!" Josie called out a fair warning. "COVER UP WHAT YOU DON'T WANT SEEN!"

Guys scrambled to dress as Josie stormed through the locker room to Coach Romano's office. She caught him just as he was about to leave.

"Hi, Coach Romano," she said, sticking out her hand to shake. "My name is Josie Geller from the Chicago *Sun-Times*. Listen, you know the local sports guy for the *Sun-Times*, Jim Lakin?"

"Sure," Coach Romano replied. "Every coach in the area tries to get Jim to cover his team."

Josie slipped a friendly arm around the coach's hefty shoulders. "Well, Coach, what would you say if I told you that I could guarantee that Jim—and every other reporter in the area—would be at the game?"

Coach's jaw dropped. "I'd say you can have whatever the hell you want!"

Ah, the power of the press! Josie thought happily. She led the coach back into his office. She had a major trade to negotiate with him.

Then Josie went home to write her story.

26

Two days later Josie's story appeared in the *Chicago Sun-Times*.

Gus came in, snapped on the light in his office, sat at his desk, and opened his newspaper to the "Life and Style" section.

And there it was, on the front page. Josie's story. Next to the article were three pictures. One was her senior picture from high school, when she was seventeen and wore glasses and braces. One was a picture of her in her Elizabethan gown at the Southglen South prom. The third was a picture of her as he knew her, a twenty-five-year-old copy editor and budding reporter.

He read the story and smiled. Who knew little Josie Geller could write like that?

Down the hall in the *Sun-Times* lunchroom, Anita and Cynthia shared a bag of microwave popcorn as they pored over every word of Josie's story. They were astounded.

"Damn! That girl can *write*!" Cynthia exclaimed.

Merkin Burns read Josie's story at his desk, highlighting his favorite parts.

Everyone in the *Sun-Times* office read the story, even before they read the front page, their horoscope, the celebrity news briefs, or the comics. They had to find out how this was all going to end.

All across Chicago newspapers flew off the newsstands.

Almost everybody waiting for the trains was reading the story. In fact, it seemed as if everyone in Chicago was reading the story.

Everyone except Sam Coulson.

Sam was at his apartment carelessly tossing pots and pans and kitchen timers into moving boxes. He was the picture of depressed: barefoot, dressed in old sweats, bleary-eyed. And he hadn't shaved since the prom. His *Chicago Sun-Times* lay on the table, still wrapped up in its clear plastic bag. Who cared what happened in Chicago anymore? He was moving to New York.

He was almost done in the kitchen. A few pot holders. Salt and pepper shakers. Refrigerator magnets. He pulled those off the refrigerator, sorting through the school notices, outdated pizza coupons, and random photos. His eyes stopped on the photo of him and Josie, covered in paint splotches as they painted a sunset together for the prom.

He plucked the photo from the fridge, stared at it a moment . . .

Then dropped it into the trash.

NEVER BEEN KISSED

by Josie Geller
Sun-Times Staff Writer

Someone once told me that to write well, you have to write what you know.

This is what I know.

I am twenty-five years old. I have never really kissed a guy. A geek to the core, I spent most of my childhood years doing extra homework I requested from the teacher.

High school was more of the same. Then, at seventeen, it seemed as if my luck was about to change. The cutest guy in school asked me to senior prom. But it turned out he had invited me as a cruel joke. I have never fully recovered.

Yes, it is embarrassing to share this

with the world. But it would be hard to explain what I learned, and how I learned it, without sharing this humiliating history.

I received an assignment, my first as a reporter, to enroll in high school as a student, to gain some insight into kids today.

Understandably, returning to high school was my worst nightmare.

What I found?

There's still that one teacher who marches to her own drummer.

Those girls are still there. The ones that, even as you grow up, will still be the most beautiful girls that you've ever seen close up.

The athletes, and the immense sense of fraternity and loyalty that they share.

The smart kids—who everyone else always knew as the brains. But who I just knew as my soul mates, my teachers, my friends.

And there's still that one guy, the one who is so perfect in every way, from the muscles in his shoulders to the way he, in his own way, struggles to uphold tradition. Southglen would not have been the same without him. High school would not be the same without him. I would not have been the same without him.

All of these things made me miserable at seventeen. But at twenty-five I finally see that this—all of this—is just the way it should be. It is all part of this thing called high school. A time in our lives that we can never truly repeat. A time that shapes us. A time that makes us who we are, for years to come.

High school. Going through it the first time helped make me who I am. But going there a second time made me see that who I am is okay. I always wanted to be "in," but seven years later, when they finally opened the door, I somehow gained the confidence to stay outside, firmly, happily.

This is not the article I was sent in to write. This is the article I needed to write. I lived a lifetime of regret after my first high-school experience, and now, after my second, my regrets are down to one.

A certain teacher was trampled in my path to self-discovery, and though this article may serve as a step, it in no way makes up for what I did to him.

To this man, you know who you are,

I am so sorry.

And I would like to add one more thing.

I think I am in love with you.

And so I propose this. As an ending to this article, and, perhaps, as an ending to this portion of my life. I, Josie Geller, will be at the state championship baseball game, where my friends, the Southglen Rams, are playing for the title.

I will stand on the pitcher's mound for the five minutes prior to the first pitch. If this man accepts my apology, I ask him to come kiss me, in front of everyone, for my first real kiss.

Five minutes may seem like a short time, but trust me, when you've been waiting twenty-five years, it's usually the last five minutes that kill you.

I went back to high school and discovered I was a loser, again. And then I discovered it wasn't so bad. I wasn't so bad. So now that I'm ready to start living the rest of my life, it would be magical if I could live the rest of it with him.

Because inside everyone is a loser afraid to be loved, and out there is the one person who can kiss us and make it all better.

• • •

In his apartment, Sam Coulson opened up the newspaper and pulled out the "Life and Style" section, but his mind was on packing, and things lost, not news features, so he did not notice the photos of his ex-student, Josie Geller, staring out from the front page, didn't stop to read her story. He carried the section over to the bookshelf in the living room and slowly, carefully, began to use the newspaper to wrap up the tarnished, dented trophies from his youth. Almost done now. Soon he'd be out of Chicago for good.

He started to dump one of the wrapped trophies into a cardboard box when something caught his eye.

Her eyes. Staring back at him from between the crumples of the paper.

27

It was just like that movie about the man who built a baseball diamond in the middle of the cornfield. *If you write it, they will come.*

Josie's story, "Never Been Kissed," seemed to have touched a tender spot in the hearts of everyone in Chicago—a spot some may have tried to deny or forget. After all, how many people could say they hadn't felt like a loser at least once in their lives?

And so the people came. To be with Josie. To pull for the loser. To cheer for the loser they once were.

And maybe witness a miracle.

Cars packed the parking lot and spilled out along the streets that led to the ballpark. People jammed the stands. Others watched from the rooftops of nearby buildings.

Many people waved their copy of the *Sun-Times* "Life and Style" section in the air. Others held up handmade signs that said things like. . .

WE LOVE YOU, JOSIE!
LOSERS MAKE THE BEST LOVERS
KISS HIM ONCE FOR ME!

The Southglen Rams baseball team—minus Rob Geller—warmed up out on the field, not quite sure what to make of the crowd.

Josie stuck her head out of the Southglen dugout and stared in amazement at the packed stands. Lights and cameras and TV reporters were everywhere. If ever she'd doubted the power of words to move people, she was a believer now. How many thousands of people had read her story and come to watch her? She couldn't guess.

She felt faint.

What had she done? She'd experienced so much humiliation in her life without even trying. Now she had gone out of her way to invite thousands of people to attend what just might be the most humiliating spectacle in the history of love.

"Wow," she whispered nervously, "it's . . . packed."

Her two best friends from her two lives—Anita

and Aldys—had insisted on being there with her.

"It's *great*!" Anita reassured Josie, her eyes glowing. "They're behind you. They feel like they know you."

Aldys squeezed Josie's hand. "It's romantic, what you're doing. And they want to be a part of it."

"Well, I'm so glad that you guys are." Josie wanted to say more, to tell them how much their support and friendship really meant to her. But she couldn't.

She was hyperventilating.

She sank down on the bench and put her head down between her ankles. Anita and Aldys grabbed the brown paper bag at the same time and handed it to her.

Josie put the reassuring paper bag over her nose and mouth and slowly breathed in and out. This was a simple procedure based on sound scientific principles. When she got excited, she began to breathe at an excessive rate and depth, thus creating a deficit of carbon dioxide in the bloodstream. Which made her feel faint. She breathed slowly into the bag, inhaling some of her own carbon dioxide, and reestablishing the balance of carbon dioxide and oxygen.

Great science experiment. But it didn't do a thing for her nerves.

She felt better by the time Coach Romano ran in from the field. She put down the bag.

"Sweet Jesus, Geller!" the coach exclaimed. "I had no idea there'd be all these TV crews here. This thing's gonna be on every station in the country!"

Josie started hyperventilating again and clutched the brown paper bag like a security blanket.

"You more than kept your end of the bargain," Coach was saying. He gave her a big, hearty, coach-like smile. "Now go out there and get 'em!"

Josie got up, and he slapped her—on the rear end.

She laughed and hugged Aldys. She was lucky the girl had forgiven her.

Then Anita hugged her, but she wouldn't let go. Josie struggled to get away, and Anita kept hugging her and pulling on her until they were both laughing hard.

Good old Anita. She always made Josie laugh.

But now it was time.

The pitcher's mound looked as if it were miles away.

A journey begins with a single footstep.

Who was responsible for that bit of wisdom? Josie wondered. A twentieth-century philosopher? Or a Chinese fortune cookie? She couldn't remember. But she took the advice and stepped out onto the field.

A roar went up from the crowd.

Josie smiled. This must be what Rob felt like when he was out there on the field, wowing the fans. She prayed to be like her little brother just once in her life and hit a home run for the crowd tonight as well.

She walked alone to the pitcher's mound, clutching a microphone, as the crowd continued to cheer and shout and stomp their feet. "JOSIE! JOSIE! JOSIE!"

When had she heard chanting like that without the "Grossie" attached? It felt really good.

When she reached the pitcher's mound, she stood until they were all quiet.

Everyone waited expectantly.

And for a moment Josie choked. *What if . . . ?*

The Loser in her began to imagine all sorts of horrible outcomes. The Loser in her told her to run like hell for the safety of the dugout and forget the whole thing. The Loser in her—

Shut up, Josie told the Loser in her. *Quit stalling and do it.*

Josie cleared her throat, wet her lips, then spoke into the microphone. "Could I have five minutes on the clock, please?"

The scoreboard clock read 5:00. Five minutes.

Hopefully (properly used), Josie began to wait.

So many employees of the *Sun-Times* stuffed the front box seats of the stadium, they could have had a staff meeting. They were eager to see how the story ended.

"I got wieners," Hyram Rigfort called out, coming back from the concession area with an armload of hot dogs. "Hot wieners!" He squeezed himself in next to Gus to watch the show. Behind him sat the investigative reporter Bruns, his hair finally growing back in from his hair-transplant story, and Henson, who had recovered enough from his skiing exposé to be down to wearing only one sling.

"I love this!" Rigfort bellowed. "*Sun-Times* readers, out here making a personal connection with one of our reporters. This is amazing, isn't it?"

Gus nodded. It was terrific for sales. But mostly, he was proud of Josie.

"Wiener?"

Gus shrugged and took one.

Rigfort started to take a bite, then gasped. "Wait a minute!" he cried, studying his own hot dog. He pulled something small and shiny out of the bun. "There's a *bolt* in my wiener!" He turned around to his reporters. "Henson! What are you doing for the next month?"

Henson looked at the hot dog and his face fell. Maybe it was time to get a job in the *Sun-Times* mail room. He had a feeling it was a whole lot safer down there.

• • •

Down on the pitcher's mound, Josie stared at the clock—2:30. Two and half minutes left.

Still time, she told herself. *Don't give up hope.* She looked for a star to wish upon, but they'd all disappeared in the glare of the stadium's night-game lights.

A flash of orange out in the bleachers caught her eye. She was touched to see the rest of the Denominators in their orange sweatshirts cheering her on. Aldys had rejoined the group, and they were laughing and shouting her name. Behind them sat the entire Southglen South marching band.

Josie forced a stoic smile.

She continued to wait.

Sam, she allowed her heart to say.

She tried to think of all the wonderful times she'd spent with him. But all she could see in her mind was the look in his eyes the night of the prom.

One minute left on the clock.

Guy and Kirsten and the gang were in the bleachers, trying to start a wave, but the crowd wasn't cooperating.

Twenty seconds.

In the *Sun-Times* box Anita slipped into a seat beside Gus. She squeezed her eyes tight, afraid to watch, and clutched his hand for dear life. Gus clutched back.

The crowd began to chant the countdown. Everyone—including every Denominator, including Guy and his friends from the Cool Table—was standing, chanting, stomping.

Josie felt the ground rumble, felt the chanted countdown pounding in her heart. . . .

Ten. Nine. Eight. Seven. Six. . . .

Josie's feet felt rooted to the spot. Her heart pounded in her brain. But she kept her head held high.

Five. Four. Three. Two. . . .

Josie stole a look at the dugout.

No Sam.

ONE!

The buzzer rang out through the stadium as the crowd fell silent. People stood frozen, stunned, unsure what to do.

Josie made one last desperate search of the stands.

No one was running toward her. No one.

No one.

The silence was as deafening as the chants had been.

Stunned, Josie dropped the microphone, and its sound reverberated in the silent stadium.

Josie closed her eyes. Tears gathered on her lashes.

Josie Grossie, whispered the demons in her mind.

Loser . . .

No, she fought back. *No!*

And then . . .

There was a commotion in the stands.

Josie's eyes flew open. And she saw him.

Sam.

His face bobbing in the sea of faces, struggling to get through.

Was he really here? Or had she conjured him with the incantations of her pounding heart?

No, it was really him, fighting his way through the crowd to reach her. And now the crowd was on its feet cheering as he burst out onto the field, as he ran toward the pitcher's mound, toward Josie.

It felt like a lifetime before he reached her, and grabbed her, and pulled her into his arms.

"Sorry I'm late," he said breathlessly. "It took me forever to get here."

Tears were streaming down her face. "I know what you mean," she said simply.

And then he kissed her. The most amazing, most waited-for kiss in the history of lovers. A kiss that would last forever.

Or at least another few minutes.

A deafening roar of approval rose from the crowd.

Overwhelmed, Anita grabbed Gus and kissed

him, too. Surprising herself. Surprising Gus, too. And then he kissed her back.

Rob Geller whooped and shouted from the dugout, wearing the ASSISTANT COACH jersey his big sister Josie had won him in this crazy crapshoot of hers.

Aldys and the Denominators cheered their brains out.

Guy and Kirsten finally succeeded in starting a wave.

Fireworks exploded above the stadium.

It felt as if all of Chicago were there.

All together.

All to celebrate.

All for one kiss.